Twelve Stories for Spring

Twelve Stories for Spring

Linda Mansfield

A Restart Communications, LLC publication

First published in the United States by Linda Mansfield.

TWELVE STORIES FOR SPRING

Copyright © 2017 by Linda Mansfield

ISBN: 978-0-9962433-4-6 (EPUB)

ISBN: 978-0-9962433-5-3 (MOBI)

ISBN: 978-0-9962433-6-0 (paperback)

ISBN: 978-0-9962433-7-7 (hardcover)

Cover art © Sunny Studio/Dollar Photo Club.

10 9 8 7 6 5 4 3 2 1

Dedication

For my immediate family, past and present:

Lloyd and JoAnne Mansfield

Karen Mansfield and Denny Duckett

Bill Shand

Thomas E. and Hazel Mae Mansfield

John D. and Madge Bruce

Evelyn Mansfield

Rhonda and Paul Cornman; Carly and Jaesa

William Shand, Martha and Raymond Lancey

Thomas and Helen Mansfield; Patty and Craig

Harold and Diane Mansfield; Kevin, Keith and Nancy

Howard and LaVonne Mansfield; Ed, Christopher and Melissa

John and Virginia Bruce; Joe and Betsy

Ed and Suzanne Bruce

Lee Bruce; Barbara, Susan, Caroline and Tom

Don and Carole Bruce; Cynthia, Douglas, Rebecca and David

David and Dolores Shand

Frances and Kenny Lundy

Bobby Shand

Sandra Shand

As for the "fringe" relatives (people who are related to these people), you're included too, but the dedication isn't supposed to be longer than the book!

Contents

Reviews

**WHAT THEY'RE SAYING ABOUT
"STORIES FOR THE 12 DAYS OF CHRISTMAS"**

"If you travel a lot, do your nerves a favor; get this book! This is the perfect 'pick it up, put it down book' to tuck into your travel bag, or have at the ready on your e-reader! Anytime of the year these cozy stories will help soothe the pains of travel and other public annoyances. Love it! I just bought two hardcover versions for Christmas gifts!" — *Kathryn, an Amazon reviewer*

"This wonderful little book is a baker's dozen packed with relaxation. I got it just before Christmas and while it would be perfect to read in quick little moments, I read it all in one night. The stories are refreshingly uplifting…perfect for a few moments with your morning cup of coffee, or in the evening with a glass of wine. Keep this in mind for next Christmas, or get a few now and share them to chase away the winter blues. Great job, Linda Mansfield!" — *Author Gloria Antypowich* (see GloriaAntypowich.com)

"This collection of short realistic stories is perfect for Christmas time. Easy reading, that will make you smile and rethink the way you live.

Very good Christmas book." — *Author Marcia Weber Martins* (see marciaweber.wordpress.com)

"'Stories for the 12 Days of Christmas' is a little like grabbing a cookie or two at a time. There is a sweetness to these stories....These are not children's stories but the language is plainspoken, easy to anticipate, and that makes the book perfect for a busy schedule....Mansfield is not writing little romantic vignettes. She is imagining ordinary people whose lives are changed by choosing love....She is offering you a Christmas break, manageable moments of connection, so that you come away refreshed and ready for more. And maybe with a little sugar high to keep you going. 'Stories for the 12 Days of Christmas' is a small book of loving reminders to be better, do better, and change your life, by choosing love. It's worth noting that it could be a gift you give to others, as well as to yourself." — *Susan Schoch, Story Circle Book Reviews*

"These light-hearted Christmas stories are very uplifting at a time when many people are depressed with the approaching holidays. Great reads while waiting for appointments or passing the time of day, with positive outcomes." — *Nena Ray*

"This collection of short stories is a perfect read for that wintery day when you just want to curl up with a blanket. I purchased it as a stocking stuffer and it is on my end table instead to be picked up and read at leisure by friends visiting. I purchased additional copies for gifts." — *Marti Humphrey*

Introduction

Indianapolis, Indiana

I've been writing newspaper and magazine articles since I was a teenager and I've edited newspapers, magazines, and other people's books, but when I tackled "Stories for the 12 Days of Christmas" I learned writing and marketing fiction is a whole different pew in the church.

Fortunately it's not hard to connect with people who know more than you do thanks to the Internet. Many of these people are generous about sharing information.

One such person is Mark Coker, founder of Smashwords. His research found the average self-published book takes about three years to become popular, if it ever does. Most don't. However, he emphasized new authors like me should not rest on their laurels but get busy writing a second book so they'll have something else to offer should their first book take off.

In one fell swoop, I was behind the eight ball again.

I have ideas for other books, but I liked the characters in "Stories for the 12 Days of Christmas," and I thought they had more stories to tell. I was curious about what they might get themselves into next.

I also like the short-story format for our busy world. A reader has to make a definite time commitment to read a novel, but he can complete a short story while waiting for a plane, at the doctor's office, in a parking lot waiting to pick up the kids, or while unwinding at bedtime. A reader can put a book of short stories down and pick it up later without having to remember much, which seems ideal for the pace and stress of daily life.

With a book of Christmas stories under my belt, I decided to advance my characters' stories chronologically into three more books to take them through spring, summer and fall. Each book will contain 13 stories. They will be part of a four-book series I call the "Two Good Feet" series in honor of my choice of cover art. The main goal of each book is to provide relaxation and stress relief for both men and women from the ages of teens through senior citizens.

Sometimes the focus will continue to be on the main characters from the Christmas book. Other times the supporting characters take center stage.

All four books will stand alone, which means a reader doesn't have to read all four books to make sense of the story lines. I don't think it's fair to have cliffhangers or "to be continued" lines.

However, if a reader does decide to read all four books, he'll get a full year in the life of these characters, or 13 novelettes consisting of four stories each.

I'd already written the first 13 stories in "Stories for the 12 Days of Christmas," but now I'd assigned myself 39 more stories to write.

You're holding stories 14 through 26 in "Twelve Stories for Spring." "Twelve Stories for Summer" will follow, and the series will conclude with "Twelve Stories for Fall."

That's a total of 52 stories, which is significant.

Why?

The late author Ray Bradbury, who wrote over 600 short stories and 27 novels, challenged aspiring authors to write a short story each week for a year, adding something along the lines of "It's not possible to write 52 bad short stories in a row."

I'm counting on him to be right, and I sincerely hope you'll enjoy these.

Linda Mansfield

LindaMansfieldBooks.com
Linda Mansfield — Author on Facebook
@RestartLMAuthor on Twitter

Please join our mailing list via the form on
LindaMansfieldBooks.com's home page
and receive a *free* short story!

Authors depend on good reviews.
If you enjoy this book, please consider posting
a short review at the outlet where you purchased it.
Thank you!

1

The End of the Road

"Mr. Simpson, lay back; you need to rest." The female voice was unfamiliar, far away, and fuzzy.

The air smelled like industrial-strength detergent, and the florescent light above the hospital bed hummed softly. Bobby Simpson heard Velcro ripping open, and felt a nurse unwrap a blood-pressure cuff from his arm. He hadn't noticed it tighten over his muscles when she pumped it up, or felt the pressure finally release. Now she was fussing with something on a pole beside the bed, out of his line of sight.

"Where am I?"

"Doves of Charity Hospital. You were in a fight in the parking lot of a bar. Two guys were after some kid's motorcycle."

"Oh, yeah," he murmured, wondering why it was hard — and painful — to speak. *And it wasn't even a Harley* he remembered, but he said nothing more that night as the pain medicine kicked in.

He slept through the rest of that night, the next morning, and most of the next afternoon. He would have slept even longer, but suddenly he needed to pee.

He hadn't needed help with that process since he was a toddler. He vaguely remembered he'd refused a nurse's suggestion for a catheter. He was embarrassed to have to ask for help, but with both arms in bandages, his left leg in a cast, and a piercing pain in his ribs, he had no choice. He felt trapped, which was almost as bad as the pain from the injuries he suffered in the fight.

The nurse took it in stride. After she left, Bobby's mind drifted back to how things had gone down yesterday. Or was it the day before yesterday?

It was spring. Bobby's thoughts weren't on love like Alfred Lord Tennyson's poem suggested, but he was open to a few beers and a little sex that afternoon in mid-March when he pulled his old Mustang into the parking lot of the small bar in northwest Arkansas.

The beer was how he liked it — cold — and it felt smooth as it went down his parched throat. The smell of hops mixed with cigarette smoke mingled in the bar's stale air. The room was dark, although several neon signs gave it spots of color and light. The jukebox was silent. The only sounds were the clinking of glasses, the mumbling of low voices, and the occasional squawks from a line of video games.

He was out of luck with the women. The girl behind the counter was wearing a wedding ring, and she wasn't interested in him. Another waitress was old enough to be his grandmother. A third was too fat for his tastes, although he wouldn't have minded taking a nap with his head nestled between her ample breasts.

Bobby knew he was good looking; he'd played that card all his life. He had thick blond hair, sapphire-blue eyes, a killer smile, and the polished approach of a professional salesman even on his worse days.

Bobby chalked up his lack of success this afternoon to the lack of opportunities.

By the time he gave up trolling for sex, he'd put away three beers and emptied the pretzel bowl. He settled up with the married bar-keeper, slipped off his stool, and headed to the parking lot out back.

The sun was blinding after the darkness of the bar, and he blinked a few times as his eyes adjusted. In stark contrast to the smoky bar, spring had erupted here via a line of Bradford pear trees standing like soldiers between the parking lot and the street. Their large, black branches supported hundreds of thinner, shorter branches, each sporting thousands of tiny bouquets of feminine white blossoms.

Earlier Bobby had noticed a skinny kid with a bad case of acne playing video games in the bar. It was a stretch to think he was 21. Now that same kid was in the bar's parking lot, sitting on a Honda motorcycle surrounded by two tough guys. One of them had his hands on the handlebars. It didn't take a rocket scientist to see what was going on.

There wasn't time to consider all the possibilities. The kid was going to get robbed of his bike faster than Bobby could down a beer. Something at Bobby's core told him he had to help.

He went to his usual weapon — his considerable charm — first.

"Hey guys, let him alone, OK?" he suggested with a wide smile. "He's only a kid."

"Mind your own business," snarled one of the thugs, who was cov-ered in tattoos.

"I'm afraid I can't do that; let's all just move along," Bobby sug-gested, still smiling.

"Why don't you move along?" the guy holding the handlebars growled, and in one motion he turned the bike over, unseating the kid.

All hell broke loose. As the petrified kid watched from the ground beside an olive-green dumpster, Bobby took and landed a few good punches until one of the thugs got the upper hand with a small knife to his rib cage.

Blood streamed from Bobby's belly. It hurt. It also made him mad.

With one motion he picked up a two by four lying beside the dumpster and cracked it over the head of the most heavily tattooed thug, who was immediately knocked unconscious. The back of the thief's head hit the metal dumpster as he buckled backwards.

By that time the kid was cowering a bit to the left and talking to a 9-1-1 dispatcher on his cell phone. The remaining thug pistol-whipped Bobby in the face before driving off quickly in an old red pickup.

The kid didn't get the license plate number. Bobby didn't either, because he and the one downed thief were lying unconscious and bleeding when the cops and the paramedics arrived. The kid was upset but unhurt. His bike was fine too, although it was still upside down.

And now Bobby was in the hospital.

Bobby wasn't sure how his leg had gotten broken, but the surgeon who set it said it wasn't a bad break. The rib injury was worse, as one of his broken ribs had punctured his lung.

Bobby was getting his days mixed up. He couldn't remember when he asked a nurse for a hand mirror, but he had been alarmed by how bad he looked. One of his brilliant-blue eyes was swollen shut. His usually beautiful face was puffy and streaked with red, green, black, and yellow bruises.

He was a mess.

The following morning he was aware of his surroundings enough to notice a nurse give him more pain medicine through his intravenous drip, which generated a thought that terrified him almost as much as the encounter with the thieves.

"Hey, I have to get out of here. I don't have insurance!" he told her.

"You're not going anywhere for a while, Honey," she replied. "You're lucky you're still alive. And the cops need to talk to you; one of the thieves didn't make it."

The thug who hit the dumpster had suffered a fractured skull and died. Bobby wasn't sure how he felt about it. He had never been involved in anyone's death before, even though this was in self-defense.

"We need to contact your next of kin," the nurse continued. "Who can we call?"

"There's nobody to call," he lied. "I don't have any relatives."

A police officer stopped by early that afternoon and took his statement. Bobby was worried when he asked a lot of questions, but later the cop said it all checked out, and he thanked him for being a Good Samaritan. He took down his cell phone number and said he'd be in touch later.

Bobby hoped there would be no later. He had to get out of this joint.

He thought about reaching for his jeans and shirt and walking out, but the emergency room workers had cut his clothes off while prepping him for surgery. He couldn't dress or stand without help anyway.

Even if he did break out of the hospital somehow, he had no car. His old Mustang was either still in the bar's parking lot, or had been towed somewhere.

He was idly channel surfing on the TV later that afternoon when a short, plump priest with dark, curly hair helped himself to the wooden chair beside Bobby's bed. With one motion the priest plopped a thin, clear-glass vase on his bedside table. It contained three daffodils and a royal-blue bow stuck onto a dark-green stick with thin, silver wire.

"Father Peter Francis McCarthy," he said with a smile of introduction, patting the bandage on Bobby's left arm. "You can call me Father Pete."

He was almost as frightening to Bobby as the thugs.

"Am I going to die?" Bobby blurted out, wondering if the priest was there to give him his last rites.

"There's nothing wrong with you that time, these good doctors, and the great doctor upstairs can't handle," Father Pete assured him. "They tell me you saved a kid during a robbery," he continued.

"Oh, I don't know. I was there."

The conversation went on from there, as the priest inquired about the pain he was feeling and the extent of his injuries. The room's beige PTAC unit under the window blew out lukewarm air occasionally, forcing them to raise their voices. Its contribution was more noisy than refreshing.

As they talked, Bobby relaxed a bit. There was something about Father Pete that made him easy to talk to, and Bobby hadn't had anyone to confide in for a long time.

Father Pete crossed his arms in front of him. "So tell me, Bobby, what do you do for a living?"

"I'm looking for work," Bobby admitted. "I have an associates degree in business from a community college, but I've been out of work for awhile. I'm on my way to Texas, because I hear you can make good money working on the oil rigs there."

"I've heard that too," Father Pete nodded. "The nurses tell me you don't have any family, Bobby," he continued. "Is that true?"

"I used to," Bobby said. "I have a mother in a nursing home in

Indiana. I had a wife and a boy in Indiana too, but we're divorced. I couldn't find work there, and my wife wouldn't leave. She wouldn't take our boy out of school there or leave her mother, who lives in the same town. I couldn't stand not working, so I lit out."

"Hmm," was all Father Pete said, but it wasn't judgmental. The older man looked him straight in his bruised eyes. "It's going to take you a while to recuperate, and if you promise not to lie to me, I'd like to help you," he said.

A flood of thoughts rushed through Bobby's mind. He looked at the bandages on his arms, the cast on his leg, and the tubing coming in and out of his body. He thought about how ghastly he looked covered in bruises. He thought about the fact that he couldn't even take a whiz without help.

He thought about the single $50 bill in his wallet, and the medical bills that were sure to come. He had no place to go when he was discharged, and no job. And he thought of Kathy and Luke, back in Indiana, and how much he wished things were different.

The only sounds were the hum of the machines attached to him and the squeak of the rubber soles on the shoes of a passing nurse in the hallway outside his door. The PTAC unit suddenly switched off, as if the universe was waiting to hear his answer.

Realizing this was his version of the end of the road, the fiercely independent Bobby Simpson made a wise decision and responded with three words that would change his life.

"OK; thank you," he murmured.

2

The Easter Guest

Mary Beth O'Leary could tell this was going to be good. Her daughter, Amanda, not yet 6, was playing "school" in the corner of Amanda's pink and white bedroom.

Mary Beth lifted her pregnant belly and maneuvered into the rocking chair in the corner of the room. She needed a break from her housework this afternoon, and this was a good excuse.

Amanda had been counting the days to Easter for two weeks. She'd circled the date on the kitchen calendar with a purple marker.

Her vivid imagination had been reaching new heights lately, and she'd been making up wild stories. She was the kind of child who'd never met a stranger, and she often talked people's ears off. Mary Beth had looked at her daughter sideways when Amanda told a long, detailed story about meeting the Easter Bunny and her children at church. At lunchtime she'd told another whopper about an imaginary Easter duck that had followed her home when she was playing at the next-door neighbor's house that morning.

Amanda called her class to attention, stepped in front of a small chalkboard easel, and drew a picture of an Easter egg with pink chalk. Then she turned once again to her students.

"Today we're going to learn about Easter," she said with a tug to her lilac leggings worn over a pink tunic top sprinkled with butter-flies. White ankle socks with pink ruffles encased her feet and were covered with red sneakers with green shoelaces. Her blond hair was in pigtails. She tried to look serious as she peered over the top of neon-green sunglasses with ladybugs on the temples.

Her students, seated on white chairs around a small, bright green, circular table, consisted of a stuffed bear she'd gotten at Radio City Music Hall last December; a small stuffed rabbit; one princess doll she'd received from her Brooklyn-based grandparents for her last birthday, and one doll curiously wearing no clothes at all.

All were paying close attention except for the rabbit, which had gotten turned around. Concentrating on her lesson, Amanda didn't notice that his head was now facing the rear, wedged between the slats on the back of the chair, his long pink ears askew.

"Easter is the day that Jesus got alive again after the soldiers killed him," she told her class seriously. "And after that he went over the rainbow bridge to be with his father. This is how it happened," she explained.

"First, Jesus and his friends had a going-away party," she told them. "They were all grown-ups, and they drank wine and ate cheese and bread," she informed them. "Then they went to a garden to hide Easter eggs, only it got to be nighttime so they couldn't have an Easter egg hunt.

"Then on Friday the soldiers did a very bad thing," she continued. "They took Jesus and they pounded nails in his hands and hung him on a cross and killed him," she said sadly, pointing to her left palm with her right index finger.

"Some ladies that knew Jesus took his body and put him in a cave so animals wouldn't get him and eat him up," she explained further.

"Three days later, on Easter Monday, the ladies went back to the cave, and Jesus was alive!" she said triumphantly. "He walked around and gave everybody Easter baskets with chocolate bunnies in them, and then he took the biggest basket with him over the bridge to give to his father in heaven. And that's why when we die, we go to heaven too!" she pronounced in conclusion.

The makeshift classroom was silent. The toys seemed impressed. Mary Beth looked at Amanda, surprised.

"Um, Amanda, we have to talk," she told her daughter after a few seconds ticked by. "That's not exactly right."

But she didn't get the chance to have that talk, because suddenly a live, full-grown Canada goose sauntered into the bedroom, looked at Amanda, and squawked at them all.

"Rodney! You have to get back into the bathroom!" Amanda admonished the goose, which looked upset that he'd missed the lesson. He tilted his long, black neck towards Amanda and cocked his head to the left, watching her every move through his bright, round, black eyes. When he saw Mary Beth, he picked up one leg at a time, balancing his weight on each leg as he weighed both himself and the situation.

"Amanda! Where did that come from?" Mary Beth cried, almost afraid of the answer. She watched, dumbfounded, as Amanda shooed the goose out of the bedroom, down the hall, and towards the bathroom that Amanda shared with her brother, Stevie.

Amanda was too busy to reply. The goose cooperated, and scurried down the hall willingly in front of her, with her stunned mother following behind.

The goose's black, webbed feet made a pattering noise on the hall's hardwood floor. When he got to the open bathroom door he flapped his large wings three times to build up steam, rose about a foot, and settled with a splash into the tub, which was almost overflowing with water. Several inches of water splashed onto the floor, which was already soaking wet. Mary Beth wondered if water was coming through the dining room ceiling below them. She was grateful Amanda hadn't added her usual bubble bath.

"Amanda Jean, what have you done?" Mary Beth said in the tone of mothers everywhere who have stumbled onto the scene of a family crime.

"I told you; Rodney came home with me this morning; he's visiting us for Easter," Amanda said patiently, surprised by her mother's reaction.

"Amanda, that is a wild animal, and he needs to be outside!" Mary Beth said in short spurts as if it was an effort to make each word follow the other one. "And look at this mess!" she continued, pointing to the small piles of goose droppings on the tile floor, the bright yellow throw rug, and the shower curtain.

"Rodney couldn't help it, Mommy; he doesn't know how to use the potty," Amanda explained patiently.

An open and almost-empty box of cereal was on the counter by the sink.

"Rodney likes cereal," Amanda informed her mother.

"I'm sure he does," Mary Beth responded. "How exactly did Rodney get into the house?"

"Well, Jenny and I were playing over at her house, and Rodney and some other ducks were playing in the water in a ditch behind her house," Amanda said. "The other ducks were kind of hissy, but Rodney was nice. We went into the house and got cereal for him, and he just followed me home."

"I'm sure he did, with you feeding him every step of the way," Mary Beth said, filling in the blanks. "Amanda, you know you shouldn't have done that. We need to take Rodney outside right now."

"But he wants to stay with me for Easter," Amanda said, pleading and batting her eyelashes like a debutante who had just spied a handsome boy in the ballroom.

"He has to stay outside," Mary Beth replied firmly. "By the way, how did you get him in the house without me seeing you?"

Amanda looked at her sneakers. She pulled her lower lip down with two fingers of her right hand, and then released it. "Well, maybe you were in the basement doing the wash," she said.

"Ah, maybe," Mary Beth replied.

Getting Rodney outside was the next challenge. Mary Beth wasn't sure the goose would remain amiable if she tried to pick him up. She knew he could peck them if he wanted to, and she didn't need more goose droppings and feathers throughout her house. She decided to go with Amanda's method.

"Go downstairs, and get that new box of cereal off the lowest shelf in the pantry," she told her daughter. "We'll try to lure him outside with it."

Surprisingly, it worked. There was a little snafu when Rodney made a wrong turn and waddled into the family room instead of the kitchen when they reached the bottom of the stairs. With encouragement from Amanda and more cereal, he got back on track. A few moments later he was eating more cereal on the deck outside the kitchen's sliding glass doors, next to a large, creamed-colored plastic planter filled with purple and yellow pansies.

Rodney seemed glad to be back outside. Mary Beth made Amanda come indoors, and together they watched as Rodney waddled down the two steps from the deck to the lawn, and pecked the grass near their magnolia tree, searching for bugs. A moment later he flapped his wings, ran a short distance, and took flight to reunite with his flock.

"Amanda, you're not to do anything like that again," Mary Beth told her daughter. "And if you do, you have to come tell me right away."

"But I did tell you, Mommy," Amanda said in her defense, her bottom lip trembling.

"OK; we'll chalk this up to a learning experience," Mary Beth said, wondering what cleaner would be best to tackle goose droppings.

Another thought dawned on her. "And now, tell me exactly what happened when you met the Easter Bunny and her children at church," she added, praying she had the stamina for the truth.

3

A Date for the Prom

Matt Stine stomped into the kitchen, flung the refrigerator door open, and reached for the dark green bottle the Stine family had used as a water bottle for two generations. He unscrewed its bright yellow lid, tipped his head back, and guzzled the whole thing until it was dry. The cool air of the refrigerator washed over his dirty baseball uniform, but it did nothing to improve his disposition. He couldn't believe Marti Cook had turned him down when he asked her to the prom.

Matt leaned against the refrigerator door and tried to regain his composure. He thought he and Marti had an understanding, but she conveniently forgot they were destined to be together.

"Shit!" he said to no one in particular as he padded over to the sink in his stocking feet, refilled the bottle, put it back in its place in the refrigerator, and slammed the door.

His grandmother, Bernice, peered up from her embroidery, gave him a look over her reading glasses, and turned back to her handiwork from her position in the brown recliner in the living room next to the kitchen. "Bad day, dear?" she asked him. "Did you lose the ball game?"

"Sorry, Grandma," Matt said. "And no, we won."

"Then what's the matter?"

"Oh, nothing," Matt said, and then relented. "Marti turned me down when I asked her to the prom."

"She did?" Bernice was surprised too. "Do you know why?"

"Yeah; she's going with Ben Hoover. She said he asked her first, and I shouldn't always expect her to be at my beck and call. What the hell does that mean, anyway?"

"It means Marti is exploring her options, and maybe you've been taking her for granted."

"Shit," Matt said. "Everybody knows we're meant to be together."

"Maybe not everybody, and watch your language."

"Sorry," Matt said as he wiped his face with the kitchen towel hanging from the handle on the oven door.

"And put that in the wash now," Bernice directed.

"Yes, ma'am," Matt said, as he took his baseball cap off his head and wadded it into a ball.

"Who are you going to take to the prom now?"

"I'm not going," Matt said flatly.

"You shouldn't miss your high-school prom." Bernice pulled a thread through her material. "I did, and I always regretted it."

"Well then you can go," Matt said without thinking.

"Really?"

"Sure! Why not?" Matt said, not fully understanding what he had proposed.

The kitchen clock on the wall chirped four times before Matt realized he'd just invited his grandmother to be his date at his high-school prom. *Oh, what the hell. What does it matter now?*

Bernice immediately gave him an out. "You don't mean that," she said. "I can't go to your prom."

Matt was warming to the idea, and he loved his grandmother. "Grandma, you wouldn't let me get turned down twice in one afternoon, would you?" he said gallantly.

And that's how Bernice Stine, age 69, got to attend Chapel Hill Area Senior High School's prom, albeit 52 years late.

As is often the case in small towns, there was a bit of history between the Stine and the Cook families.

It was called "The Spring Dance" instead of the prom at the time, but Bernice had missed the biggest social event of her senior year in high school after a tiff with Marti's grandfather, Charlie Cook. He'd asked her to go with him a few weeks before the big event, but she'd declined because she knew there wasn't enough money in the household budget to afford material for a new dress. She'd been too embarrassed to explain her reasoning, and Charlie had held it against her from that point forward.

They eventually met and married other people. Years later, they nodded to each other politely when their paths crossed, like two adversaries acknowledging each other's presence as they passed.

Bernice went to beauty school after high school and still ran one of the two beauty shops in town. Charlie went to college in another state, but when he was in his forties he returned to his hometown to teach history at the high school. He was set to retire in a few weeks, at the end of the school year.

They'd both lost their spouses. Nancy Cook died of cancer last winter. Bernice lost her husband the previous summer under suspicious circumstances, although the coroner ruled he'd had a heart attack while fighting a hay fire on their farm.

Bernice's reaction to the idea of finally going to a prom had a definite cycle. It started with disbelief, and grew into wondering what it would be like. She went through a period where she was adamant she would not go, and finally decided she would when Matt insisted he wanted her to. At the end she was as excited as a schoolgirl, which transferred over to her clients at the beauty shop and her women's circle at church.

One Saturday afternoon before the big day Bernice and her best friend, Sylvia, sat on hard plastic chairs in front of a slanted counter-top at the fabric shop in the next town, pouring over dress patterns before selecting one they both loved. After considerable debate they also selected the required fabric in a cornflower blue that matched Bernice's eyes, and white lace to go over the stand-up collar and the bodice. The ladies in their circle forego their study of the book of John to work on the dress, which turned out beautiful. Bernice would wear the black pumps she'd bought two Christmases ago, and carry a small black purse she borrowed from her daughter-in-law, Matt's mom.

Matt didn't rent a tux, but he looked like a million bucks in his one and only suit as he pinned a waxy, white orchid corsage on his grand-mother's dress before they left for the prom. Matt's mother insisted on taking photos of them in front of the big lilac tree in the front yard. As they waited for her to figure out which settings to use on her camera, the tree's rich fragrance increased the feeling of formal-ity and luxury. When she was finally satisfied, the couple left in a sil-ver BMW Matt had borrowed for the occasion from one of his dad's business associates.

"Matt, thank you for doing this for me; it's a dream come true," Bernice told him, settling into the car's plush upholstery. "You are such a fine young man to do this for your grandma."

"Ah, it'll be fun," Matt said, and as the night went on he found the white lie was true. His grandmother was a hit. He had no idea she would remember all the steps to the dances of her youth, or that she had learned a few new ones at the Y in preparation for her big night. Bernice forgot her arthritis and her bad knee through all the excitement. She danced both slow and fast dances with Matt, and both were pleased when Brendan Bruce, the catcher on the baseball team, cut in once.

As is true for most proms, social revelations occurred that night in the ladies' room. There were a few girls inside chatting noisily when Bernice entered. She was glad the volume of the band was much lower in the restroom, as it was a little too loud for her comfort in the gym. There were two levels of music in the restroom, as the volume went up each time the outer door opened.

Marti was at the sink, applying more mascara. She looked lovely, but she also didn't look like she was having a good time.

"Is everything OK, dear?" Bernice asked her as she washed her hands.

"Sure, Mrs. Stine," Marti responded without conviction, watching her via the mirror above the sink.

Bernice loved to play matchmaker, and she was good at it. "Are you having a good time with Ben? I am with Matt," she said.

"Well...." Marti's voice trailed off.

Bernice was born 69 years ago, not yesterday, and she could read between the lines. "Don't do anything you don't want to do, Marti," she advised. "You're a lady, and you deserve to be treated like one."

"I know, Mrs. Stine. Thank you," Marti said and changed the subject. "You look lovely."

"Thank you, dear; so do you," Bernice said, adding, "Matt said so too."

"He did?"

"Of course; he thinks the world of you."

"Thank you, Mrs. Stine," Marti repeated, and pursed her lips to apply additional lip gloss.

"Back to the dance floor I go!" Bernice said with a smile.

Matt was waiting for her at the punch bowl when she returned to the gym, which didn't look much like a gym with its crepe-paper decorations and colorful floodlights. She was more than a little surprised to see Charlie Cook standing beside him. He wore a black suit and looked distinguished.

"Hi, Grandma!" Matt said when she walked up to him. "Mr. Cook is one of the chaperones tonight, and he asked if you were behaving yourself."

"Oh, I'm having a wonderful time," Bernice told them both, and turning to Matt, added, "I saw Marti in the ladies' room, and I'm sure she would like you to ask her to dance."

"I doubt that," Matt said flatly. "She's here with Ben Hoover."

"Are you going to let him get the girl you want?" Bernice asked him. "Where is your backbone?"

"OK, OK! I give up," Matt said, and added softly, "Would you please excuse me?"

"Certainly!" Bernice and Charlie chimed in unison.

One song ended, allowing them a few moments of quiet.

"You look beautiful tonight," Charlie told Bernice.

"Thank you," Bernice said. "I can't believe I'm at a prom with my grandson, but I'm having a wonderful time."

"You mentioned backbone, and I guess I need a little of that now too," Charlie said. "You never told me why you turned me down for our own dance so many years ago."

"I'm truly sorry," Bernice said honestly. "I was embarrassed. Times were tough, and I didn't want to ask my family for money for a new dress. It seemed easier not to go, but I wanted to."

"Really?" Charlie asked.

"Really," Bernice confirmed.

"Well, we need to make up for lost time then," Charlie said. "May I have this dance?"

Bernice felt like Cinderella when she and Matt drove home in the borrowed BMW, and Matt was whistling when he pulled the car into the driveway. Bernice had a date with Charlie for bingo at the VFW the following Friday night. Marti had promised to be in the stands at Matt's next baseball game.

Matt's bedroom was on the first floor. Bernice still lived on the family farm on the outskirts of town, but since her husband's death she often stayed in her son's guest room upstairs, like she was doing tonight.

"Thank you for a night I'll always remember," Bernice told Matt as she carried her shoes in her right hand and reached for the stairs' banister with her left. "You were so nice to take me."

"Glad to do it, Grandma; it worked out great for me too," Matt said with a smile.

4

The Transformation
Of Jeb Mitchell

With two loud snores that transitioned into snorts, 17-year-old Jeb
Mitchell turned sideways on the shiny white PVC recliner beside
what remained of the campfire in his backyard, trying to get comfortable despite his 360-pound bulk. He woke himself with the effort,
and tried to focus out of his bleary blue eyes as the sun rose. The
birds weren't awake yet, but tulips and daffodils planted by a previous
homeowner nodded in the stiff breeze of early spring.

It must have been a good St. Patrick's Day party last night. He
already had a headache from his hangover.

He blinked a couple of times, trying to focus like a patient at the
eye doctor's office who just received numbing eye drops. He tilted
his head to the right, willing his brain to find any gear and engage.

He realized he was cold, and flipped the hood of his Cincinnati
Bengals hoodie over his messy, long blond hair.

He thought about putting his shoes on, and noticed a hole in the big toe of his left crew sock. The sock had been white once, but was dull beige now.

Ignoring it, he slipped into his canvas shoes. Black with orange flames, they had fallen off sometime during the night.

Jeb was surprised his father hadn't forced him to go to bed in the room he shared with his brother Danny, two years his junior. The trio had moved to the brick ranch outside of Louisville, Kentucky, three years ago after Mike and Laurie Mitchell finally divorced after years of arguments. Laurie got the family's tri-level in the divorce. The brothers had their own bedrooms there, but they had to share when they stayed with their dad.

The family's dogs, Duke and Lug, were awake now too, but both remained flat on the ground next to what little heat remained from the campfire.

Jeb teetered to his feet and stretched, thankful it was Saturday and there was no school. Jeb was not a fan of school.

He needed a hot shower and he wanted it immediately. It was still early enough that the neighborhood was quiet.

He could see the street and the neighbor's house across the cul-de-sac. A flash of white shined on the sidewalk across the street. His first thought was that he'd overdone it last night, and was about to have a heart attack and meet an angel.

It was Caroline Brady instead. She lived across the street and she was in his algebra class, but they'd never met.

Caroline turned towards her front door, returning from an early-morning run. Her long legs extended from tiny white shorts, and her lilac bra showed through her skimpy white T-shirt. Her shoulder-length, brunette hair was tied up in a ponytail, and she was wearing earphones.

To Jeb, she was a vision. He wondered why he'd never noticed her before. Her mom was a bit of a pain, but Jeb was willing to overlook Caroline's breeding since it had given her those legs.

Two days later Jeb gave Caroline another once-over during algebra class. He did the same every other day that week and the next. By the end of the second week he was smitten with a young woman whom he'd never even talked to.

The following Tuesday he got his chance as the students filed out after class. He timed things right, and reached the door as she did.

"After you," he said gallantly. "Caroline, is it? We're neighbors."

"Ah, yes," she said dismissively, although she did give him a small smile because she was raised to be polite.

Although they were connected geographically, Jeb knew they were far apart socially.

That night he looked himself in the bathroom mirror and decided to make some changes. He'd known for a long time that he needed to lose weight. What he hadn't realized was his appearance was slovenly at best.

The next morning he started a daily exercise regimen in the garage consisting of push-ups and sit-ups followed by weightlifting.

He called his mom and asked her to make an appointment for him with her hairdresser when he would visit the following weekend.

His mom was overjoyed.

Jeb almost backed out when he entered the salon that Saturday. It had an industrial look and wasn't overly feminine, but he felt like a fish out of water when he walked up to the receptionist and told her he had a 2 o'clock appointment with Toni.

Toni turned out to be a short woman only slightly older than he was. Jeb was sure he'd made a big mistake as soon as he saw her spiked blue hair. She was dressed in black from head to toe. Her main accessories were a huge brown belt and matching knee-length boots.

But she was kind, and up to the task. "What can I do for you today, Jeb?"

"I need to look conservative," he sighed.

"We can do that," she said confidently. "Would you like to look at some magazines to get ideas?"

Jeb had come this far, and he wasn't a coward. He riffled through the pages of just one magazine and pointed to a male model in an ad for sunglasses. "Something like that," he said.

"Will do," Toni replied.

Within minutes most of Jeb's hair lay on the floor. He felt strange when Toni shaved off his stubble and most of his sideburns, but he melted like a baby when she massaged his head after a shampoo.

When she was finished, the transformation was remarkable.

"You're good-looking," Toni announced, without even trying to hide her surprise. "Now that you're cleaned up, your blue eyes are amazing. Remember you'll need a haircut at least once a month from now on," she informed him, and then passed him along to a manicurist.

That went fine until that woman reached for a bottle of clear nail polish.

"No polish," Jeb ordered in a firm tone that made her put it back in the rack immediately.

Looking in the mirror afterwards, Jeb knew he looked good. His mother's reaction gave him added confidence. He needed that when Danny and his dad got a look at him, but he took their teasing in stride.

"You look like a preppy," his dad said without thinking.

"Either that or a puppy that's been to the groomers," was Danny's contribution.

The big question was what would Caroline think.

"Is that you, Jeb?" she said on Monday after class. "I see you've made some great changes!"

"Yes! Thank you," Jeb said as he looked her straight in the eye, although he would never admit he'd done it all for her.

She suddenly changed the subject. "Jeb, where do you go to church?" she asked.

"I don't go," he admitted, caught off guard.

"Well, I'm a member of Bethel Methodist Church, and we're having a work project this Saturday at church," she said. "We're baking about 3,000 chocolate-chip cookies to sell to raise money for our summer service project in Appalachia."

"What?"

"My church's youth group is raising money for a trip to Appalachia this summer, where we spend a week working on projects for families in the area who need help," Caroline explained. "It's fun!"

That's how Jeb found himself getting up at 6 a.m. the following Saturday, making his way to the large kitchen in the basement of Bethel Methodist Church, donning a hair net and filmy plastic gloves, and plopping cookie dough on cookie sheets with a utensil a bit smaller than an ice cream scoop.

Jeb didn't mind, because Caroline was doing the same job on the other side of a long metal table with a scratched aluminum top.

As they worked, they got acquainted. Jeb learned both Caroline and her younger sister were avid tennis players and were good enough to be in contention for college scholarships.

Jeb had never played tennis, and college hadn't occurred to him. He had vague ideas about trying to open a comic store after high school, or perhaps running a car wash. College wasn't on his radar, but he didn't admit that to Caroline.

Jeb found he enjoyed baking. The rich scent of the chocolate and vanilla along with the camaraderie of the group made it fun. Jeb knew a few of the other kids, although he had never hung out with any of them.

"Do you think you'll go along on our service project this summer?" Caroline asked him.

"I don't know; I'd like to," Jeb replied, and was surprised to realize it wasn't a fib. "When is it?"

"The last week in July," Caroline said. "If we don't raise enough money, we'll all have to chip in. That's why the cookie drive is so important. We have other projects lined up too, but this one is usually our best money-maker."

The conversation drifted off for a bit, and they worked in companionable silence.

"Only 300 more, and we're done!" announced Philip Barker, one of the adult leaders.

The cookie sale was a big success. A car wash, a paper drive, and a smaller hoagie sale brought in more revenue for the church group too.

Jeb was a part of it all, and more often than not Caroline was by his side. He hadn't gotten the nerve to ask her on a real date yet, but he felt like he was on the right track since he hadn't grossed her out or caused her to react in disgust towards him yet. Jeb felt that was the least he could expect due to the example set by his parents.

His self-improvement project was proceeding. He still had a way to go with his diet, but cutting back on the beers was helping. He hadn't smoked anything, legal or illegal, since his day at the beauty salon, and he found he was hitting his schoolbooks a little more than his comic books and video games. He still wasted a lot of time listening to country music on the boom box in the backyard, but he hadn't been drunk since the St. Patrick's Day party.

Everyone noticed.

"I like the changes you're making, son," his father told him one night over a dinner of take-out pizza. "What caused them all?"

"Jeb is in love with the girl across the street," Danny blurted out.

"Is that so?" Mike inquired.

"Shut up, Danny!" Jeb barked, but he didn't deny it.

"Well they seem to be good people, even if we did have a little trouble with them last Christmas," Mike pointed out. "The mom came around eventually."

Across the street, Caroline was undergoing similar inquisitions.

"You've been spending time with Jeb Mitchell, haven't you?" her mother, Deb, asked her one afternoon.

"He's not so bad, Mom," Caroline pointed out.

"What college is he planning on attending?" Deb wanted to know.

"I'm not sure," Caroline answered. "But he's been going to youth group at church, and I think he's going to go with us to Kentucky this summer."

"Hmm," was all Deb said in response.

Finally, Jeb decided to ask Caroline out. He wasn't sure where they should go or how he should go about asking her. He'd never dated much.

After a great deal of thought, he decided to ask her to go with him to the Kentucky Derby on the first Saturday in May. He figured all girls were goofy over horses, which might make her say yes.

She never seemed to be alone at school, so he thought a church youth group meeting might be his best opportunity. Almost a week passed before he finally got the chance after the session, when they were both in the parking lot. He had driven his old Ford Focus there, but she was waiting for her mother to pick her up.

It was now or never.

"Do you want to go with me to the Kentucky Derby?" he blurted out, with no introduction.

"Oh, hi Jeb," she said, surprised. "I didn't see you there."

Jeb looked at his feet. He knew he should look her square in the eye, but that was asking too much.

"Do you want to go with me to the Kentucky Derby?" he repeated, his head still down.

"Um; when is it?" Caroline said.

"It's always the first Saturday in May," Jeb responded. He thought everyone knew that fact.

"I've never been to it; I guess I could go," Caroline said, game for a new experience.

"OK; I'll pick you up at noon that day," Jeb said, finally raising his head. He'd rehearsed the sentence, so he didn't know why it came out with the words all running together.

In the days ahead, Jeb thought about what he'd wear. He cleaned his car inside and out, and with his father's help, he purchased grandstand tickets from a guy his dad knew. The night before the big day, he laid out clean tan Dockers and a green polo shirt to wear to the track.

That Saturday morning he was in Caroline's driveway at 11:45 a.m. He sat in the driveway awhile, waiting for her to come out, but when she didn't appear he realized he'd need to ring the doorbell.

Her mother answered, gave him a fake, terse smile, and announced, "Caroline, your date is here."

Jeb would have been offended but he forgot her tone immediately when Caroline appeared in the foyer. She was dressed to the nines in a white linen suit, sandals with rather high heels, and a funny white hat complete with a navy-blue veil.

"Wow!" he said in appreciation, and Caroline smiled.

Unfortunately, things went downhill from there.

Perhaps it was the newness of the situation, or the fact that Caroline was so dressed up, but Jeb couldn't think of a thing to say to her in the car. She tried to break the silence a couple of times, but gave up when her questions only generated one-word replies.

Even though he knew the route well, Jeb took the wrong exit to Churchill Downs and they were stuck in traffic for 20 minutes.

The heel of Caroline's right shoe broke off as they walked from the parking lot to the grandstand. Jeb wasn't sure if it was appropriate or not, but he put his arm around her shoulders so she didn't teeter as much.

Caroline couldn't walk without lurching so they waited for the handicapped shuttle, which was a golf cart driven by a heavyset man. Jeb was glad for the opportunity to be close to her. She was wearing perfume, and its spicy scent mingled exotically with the citrus smell of her shampoo.

They made their way to their seats, passing beautiful hanging baskets and planters holding colorful spring flowers. There was an air of excitement among the crowd, which grew larger as more people arrived. Many were dressed formally. A few were comical. One man wore a cardboard cutout of a horse and a hat made out of a silver loving cup filled with orange plastic carrots.

Jeb had studied the day's program online and had his picks committed to memory. He was surprised when Caroline declined to bet at all, murmuring something about not wanting to contribute to a sport that considered horses as commodities.

When she said that, Jeb wished he were in the infield with his buddies, like he'd been in the past.

He tried to salvage the situation with food.

"Do you want a hot dog?" he asked, forgetting she was a vegan.

"Oh!" he said when he remembered. "I'll get you a salad and a soft drink instead." He knew mint juleps were the drink of choice here, but he wasn't old enough to order one of them.

As he stood in a long line for the refreshments, Jeb wondered how he could turn the tide.

Caroline accepted the salad and beverage politely, and excused herself to go to the ladies' room. She lurched away, and Jeb looked out over the track with an audible sigh.

As the card progressed, the crowd got more excited as the time for the Derby grew closer. Caroline and Jeb both tried to make the best of things, but Caroline secretly wished she'd gone to tennis practice. Jeb wondered if there was any way to salvage the day. He also thought about his recent journey towards self-improvement, and wondered if it had been a waste of time.

To make matters worse, he hadn't cashed in a ticket yet.

When it finally came time for the Derby, Caroline seemed to be a little more enthusiastic. She watched intently as the 3-year-old horses, their jockeys, and their outriders paraded in front of the grandstand. The colors of the jockeys' silks, the well-dressed crowd, and the bright green of the turf course and the lawns shouted "Spring!" as the field made its way onto the loamy dirt surface of the main track. Caroline and Jeb both sang "My Old Kentucky Home" along with the crowd. They were too far away to see the starting gate well.

After all the build up, it was over in about two minutes. Neither of them could see the finish line thanks to a huge man in the row in front of them. He was wearing a white-and-blue polka-dotted suit, and his arms flayed wildly as he cheered his winner home.

Jeb and Caroline watched the replay on a TV behind the grandstand seats, near the betting counters.

Jeb's Derby pick finished next to last.

"Jeb, I think this ticket might be good," Caroline said shyly as she drew a stub from her white straw handbag.

"When did you make a bet?" Jeb asked, dumbfounded.

"While you were in line for refreshments. It took forever, so I had time."

Jeb looked at the stub she held in her manicured hands. "Caroline! You got the Trifecta!" he said, astonished.

"I did, didn't I?"

"I didn't think you knew what a Trifecta was!" Jeb continued, amazed.

"I don't," she replied. "I told the man at the ticket counter I'd like a Trifecta because it sounded exotic. He said I needed to give him three numbers, so I gave him the code to the lock on my gym locker."

She cashed her ticket, collecting $3,445.60 before they lurched to the escalator and the line for the handicapped shuttle to the parking lot.

5

A Penny from Heaven

Minerva Stewart stepped around the piles of moving boxes in the living room of her rambling farmhouse and headed for its wide front porch. Her bright-yellow fabric handbag was slung over her left shoulder and she held a tall glass of lemonade in her right hand. It was warm for Pennsylvania in April, and she needed a break from packing. Since her strong work ethic made her feel guilty when she took even the slightest break during the day, she'd brought her handbag with her to the porch to clean it out while she rested.

Minerva took a sip, set her glass on a white wicker coffee table, and lowered herself into a matching loveseat sporting blue-and-white gingham cushions. She unzipped her handbag, turned it over, and dumped the contents out on the coffee table beside her drink.

There were stray receipts and notes she'd written to herself, a couple of candy wrappers left over from her pastor's particularly long sermon last Sunday, tissues that had seen better days, and even a grocery store circular that had come in the mail. Minerva dumped the trash into a small, white-wicker wastebasket beside the love seat.

Her wallet was especially heavy with spare change, so she dumped it out on the coffee table too. She'd take most of it back into the house later and make a deposit in the old ceramic piggy bank on a shelf in the living room, as was her practice.

"Ma! Where are you?" she heard her adult son, Michael, call out.

"On the porch!"

In a few seconds Michael appeared. "What are you doing?"

"Just going through stuff in my bag," Minerva answered. "I needed a break."

"I know downsizing and moving are hard; you never liked change," Michael said. Although he didn't mean to, it sounded like he was patronizing her. At 79, Minerva hated to be patronized.

"No, I don't like change; I prefer folding money," she answered with a wry smile as she looked at the pile of quarters, dimes, nickels, and pennies on the table in front of her.

"Good one, Mom," Michael replied, appreciatively. His mother was getting forgetful, but often she was still sharp as a tack. "Can you stop for a minute and show me the chair you want me to fix?"

"All right," Minerva agreed, rising to go inside with him. "I'll finish this a little later."

While the pair was inside, a large crow swooped down from one of the old oak trees in front of the farmhouse and perched on the porch railing, attracted by the shiny collection of coins sparkling in the sunlight. He cocked his beady eyes like he did when searching for the biggest worm in the garden right after a storm. He hopped onto the coffee table, picked up a coin in his beak, hopped back onto the railing, and flew back into the oak tree with the stealth of the thief that he was. He still had a gleam in his eye as he dropped the coin into twigs on the side of the nest he was building with his mate, high in the branches of the large tree.

Minerva returned in a few moments. As she was putting a smaller selection of coins back into her wallet, she discovered her loss.

"Where's my lucky penny?" she asked herself, alarmed.

The crow had stolen one of her most prized possessions. Her late husband, Ralph, had given her that penny on their first date when they were both 16 after he'd mustered up the courage to ask her to accompany him to the county fair.

Ralph had gotten the penny in his change when he bought her a soft ice cream cone at one of the booths. Neither of them knew what to say to each other that night, and the shiny penny had been a conversation starter since poor honest Abe was headless on this particular coin. His jacket and collar plus a bit of the bottom of his beard could be seen, but the rest of his head was gone. Somehow it had missed the quality-control folks at the U.S. Mint.

Minerva had kept the penny in her wallet all these years for good luck. She'd rubbed it on her wedding day, she'd rubbed it during the early stages of labor when she was giving birth to Michael, she'd rubbed it when Ralph and she were waiting for the bank officer to give them a loan to buy the farm, and for every other major event in her life from that day on. She'd wrapped it in her best handkerchief during Ralph's viewing and funeral and carried it in her hand instead of her wallet so it was even closer to her than usual. She'd rubbed it a few times in these last few months too as she got ready to sell most of her possessions and the farm and move into a condo downtown.

She knew it was only a penny, but like the farm it was part of her history. Now the penny was gone. Combined with the downsizing and the plan to put the farm up for sale and move, Minerva felt like everything she had was slipping away.

Michael talked a lot about how much easier her life would be without so much to take care of, and Minerva supposed that was true. But she also suspected Michael wanted his own life to be a little easier without worrying about her alone on the farm, and having to help her with repairs now that Ralph was gone. The bottom line was it was all a precursor to Minerva dying someday herself, and Minerva did not want to dwell on that scenario. She wasn't enjoying downsizing.

Michael's wife had divorced him when their daughter Wanda was only a baby, signing away all rights to her child. Wanda was now 12. There were a few things Minerva would keep for her so they would stay in the family, but a 12-year-old girl wasn't old enough to be interested in a lifetime of china or all the quilts Minerva had stitched over the years, let alone the antique furniture that filled every room of the farmhouse.

The thought of strangers taking the furniture she'd dusted and used all these years didn't sit well with Minerva. Michael suggested taking photos of everything for posterity's sake, and he'd been doing that with his digital camera, but it didn't help Minerva's feeling that her entire life was being discarded.

As silly as it seemed, that penny was a connection to Ralph. They had worked hard to get this farm in the first place, and they'd continued to work hard to keep it. Some years the crops weren't what they'd hoped. Other years the prices they got for their crops and their livestock were lower than they expected. Ralph broke his leg one spring and Minerva herself had done all the plowing and planting. They'd scrimped, saved, and worked hard to get the farm in the black when it had fallen into the red. Now it seemed like Minerva was losing it all, and the game of life — or at least the game of her life — was over.

She'd been packing for a month now. Her friend Judy helped a little, but there was still a lot to do. Michael had already selected and purchased her condo downtown, and she was going to move into it next Thursday. She'd already be settled there when the auction was held at the farm this summer, and then the bulk of her worldly possessions would belong to someone else.

Michael, Wanda, and Judy all tried to be positive, and they talked a lot about how much fun she'd have in this next chapter of her life. Judy wondered aloud if Minerva would make enough money at the auction to be able to go on a cruise with her next winter.

Minerva knew Clara Hippensteele hadn't made out well at her auction a year ago. Clara used to live two farms over, before she downsized and moved off her farm to Florida. Her furniture, antiques, and dishes brought low prices at her auction, and less than six months later she was dead. Of course she'd been battling cancer for at least 10 years, but Minerva was convinced the sale had something to do with her neighbor's demise.

Everyone except Minerva thought downsizing was the thing to do.

When Thursday arrived, it came with a cold front that brought morning showers. Minerva moved slowly through her morning routine, but she was ready when Michael arrived to take her to the condo.

"Are you ready, Mom?" he asked, kindly.

"I guess," she said. She tried to give him a smile, but was unsuccessful.

"I know it's hard," he agreed. "It's hard for me too. I can't imagine how hard it is for you."

"Thank you, son," Minerva said, looking up in an attempt to keep her tears from spilling out. "I keep wondering what Ralph would think of this," she added. "We worked hard to keep this farm."

"I know you did," Michael said sympathetically as he opened the farmhouse's heavy front door and they passed over the threshold.

Minerva turned the key in the lock, turned around, and followed Michael toward the porch's stairs. As she walked along the sidewalk, she passed a flowerbed she'd tended for many years. The crocuses were over but the daffodils were going strong, swaying in the breeze like trumpets heralding her departure. They had frilly, bright yellow centers the color of egg yolk. The tulips were also blooming. The pistils were exposed on several of them, showing waxy yellow stigma that looked like a snail she should spray for, had she had the time. The flowers showed drops of the earlier rain. Coupled with the wet mulch, the flowerbed gave off a heavenly perfume mixed with an earthy, rich aroma.

Minerva slowly proceeded along the sidewalk. She was under one of the property's large oak trees and almost to the car when something dropped from the sky and hit her square on the head.

"What's that?" she said, startled.

Whatever it was bounced onto the sidewalk in front of her. Minerva stooped and picked it up without thinking, peered into her right hand, and was astonished to see a penny containing a headless rendition of America's 16th president.

Her penny had fallen from the bird's nest high in the tree at that very moment, but Minerva had a different story.

"It's my penny from heaven!" she told Michael. "It's my sign Ralph is fine with the move, and things are going to be OK!"

And so they were.

6

A Broken Promise

"I'm so sorry; I can't!"

Tears streaming down her made-up face, Cassie Hess turned from her fiancé, dropped her bouquet of white daisies, picked up the train of her bridal gown with one hand, and ran down the aisle of the small church and out its wooden double doors.

Everyone looked shocked, especially the fiancé and the pastor, who had just asked Cassie if she'd take Rob Jones to be her lawfully wedded husband.

Jim Hess, the father of the bride, shook his head and suppressed a smile. To his way of thinking, his daughter had just saved herself from the biggest mistake of her young life. He'd had reservations about the marriage since the couple announced their engagement at the big family get-together the day after Christmas. He didn't think it was because he was losing his only daughter. There were things about Rob Jones he just didn't like.

Jim was sitting on the end of the aisle in the first pew on the right, beside his ex-wife, Cassie's mother. He could feel her shock. His current wife, Chris, was right behind him in the second pew.

No one was sure what to do.

Jim ran his right hand through his brown hair, freshly cut after a trip to the barber for this occasion. The smell of candle wax and flowers permeated the room. The sun streamed through the large stained-glass windows behind the altar, as though nothing had happened to rock the small Ohio community on this first Saturday morning in June.

Jim was pretty sure there was nothing in the bridal magazines on how to handle this one, so he didn't think he'd be lambasted later for a lack of etiquette. In a few steps he was at the altar, where he put his hand on the shoulder of Cassie's intended.

"I'm sorry, Rob," he said quietly.

He exchanged a few words with the pastor, who then addressed the congregation.

"I'm sorry, folks; there has been a change of plans," the pastor said. "Marriage is a holy institution and not something to be taken lightly. If someone is not committed to the partnership, it is best to not enter into it. We trust God will help both Cassie and Rob. I ask you all to remember them both in your prayers."

Jim hated public speaking about as much as death itself, but he knew there were practical questions needing answers.

He also knew he'd signed on the dotted line agreeing the caterer's fees were non-refundable. He made his living driving a truck, and he'd been saving for this wedding as soon as the couple had announced their engagement.

"If you all want to proceed to Fellowship Hall for the reception, at least you can have lunch," he told the congregation. "If you have an envelope or a present with you, please keep it or return it. If you've already sent a gift, it will be returned to you. We're very sorry."

With that, Jim followed the same path as his daughter had taken, although at a slower pace, and left everyone behind him to figure out their next steps on their own.

He found Cassie vomiting beside her Mazda. Rob's Chevy, which had been decorated with crepe-paper streamers, a "Just Married" sign in the rear window and a string of tin cans at the rear bumper, was parked beside it.

"OK Cassie; it's going to be OK," he assured her. Her medium-length brown hair had been in an up-do that now drooped onto her shoulders.

"Mom is going to kill me, but I just couldn't do it, Dad," she choked out, wiping her red nose with the side of her right hand.

"I'll take care of your mother; you get a hold of yourself," Jim told her, and gave her a hug despite the vomit on the front of her bridal gown.

"It's just stress," Cassie said. "I should know. I'm a nurse, remember?"

Jim felt more than heard his wife, Chris, behind him.

"Chris will take you back to your apartment and help you get cleaned up," he directed. "I'll get there as soon as I can."

"What about Rob?" Cassie asked. "He probably wants to kill me."

"Rob will be OK," Jim said. "And if he isn't, I'll handle it."

Chris put her arm around Cassie's shoulders and pointed her towards their car, but it was too late. Jim's ex-wife, Gloria, had arrived. Their son, Jim Jr., was right behind her.

"Cassie! This is humiliating!" she said. "It's just cold feet! You get back in there and apologize, and then get married!" she ordered her daughter. "What will everyone think?"

"Oh Gloria, give it a rest," Jim told her. "Think of your daughter for once, OK?"

"What about all the money we spent on this wedding?" she said angrily. "I paid for part of it, you know."

"Oh, Gloria," Jim repeated. "Why don't you go inside and have a party with your side of the family? I know you won't associate with any of my folks. And you might tell the DJ to pack up, too," he added. "Jim Jr., why don't you take your mother back into the church?"

Julia Bradshaw, Cassie's maid of honor, reached them next.

"Cassie, what do you want me to do?" she said, worried about her best friend.

"I'll be OK; please tell everyone I'm sorry," Cassie said.

Jim, Cassie, and Chris all turned and headed towards Jim's car. He had thought he would stay at the church a little longer to try to smooth things over, but it looked like he had better drive the two women back to Cassie's condo instead.

When they arrived, Chris helped Cassie get out of her gown. She returned to Jim in the living room while Cassie took a quick shower.

"What should we do next?" she asked her husband, who had popped on the TV and was watching the Cincinnati Reds game.

"I don't know; it's all virgin territory to me," Jim admitted.

Cassie returned a bit later, wearing jeans and a green tunic top. Her brown eyes were bloodshot, but at least she wasn't crying anymore. Jim switched the TV off, even though the Reds were winning.

"I have to get out of here," Cassie told them. "I can't face anybody right now."

"Where do you want to go?" Jim asked.

"I don't know."

After a few minutes of conversation, they decided Jim would drive

Cassie and Chris to a hotel in the next town where the three of them would spend the night. After Jim dropped them off, he would go home and pack what he and Chris would need before he joined them later that afternoon. They didn't want Cassie to be alone.

That was the plan, but nothing was going to plan that day.

Before they could leave the condo, Rob knocked on the front door. He had taken the jacket of his tux off, and undone his tie. He looked hurt and angry. A bump on his jaw pulsed in and out.

Jim and Chris knew they should leave the pair alone. They stepped onto the condo's small front porch, but Jim cracked the front door so he could hear them if the conversation should turn ugly. He hadn't been overly impressed with Rob from the beginning, and he wasn't sure what Rob was capable of doing when spurned.

"Cassie, why don't you want to marry me?" Jim heard Rob say. "Don't you love me?"

"I do love you, Rob, but I don't love you enough," she told him, tears once more sliding down her face. "I thought I did, but I don't."

"Do you think it might just be cold feet?" Rob asked hopefully. "We can fix this, Cassie."

"No, we can't, Rob," Cassie said, handing him her engagement ring. "I'm not the girl for you. You deserve to find somebody who will give you everything you want in life, and I just can't."

"So this is it?" Rob asked.

"I'm afraid so, and I'm very sorry," Cassie replied. "I hope someday you'll be able to forgive me."

"I'll never forgive you," Rob replied coldly. He turned, stomped out the front door, ignored the couple that was going to be his in-laws until about an hour ago, and left.

Jim and Chris went back inside to find Cassie standing in the living room.

"I feel guilty I hurt him, but I feel relieved too," she told them.

Jim and Chris hugged her, and the three of them stood and rocked for a few minutes in a group hug.

"So what else do you want to do today?" Jim asked innocently, and all three of them laughed.

"I liked the idea of going to a hotel," Chris said. "We can relax awhile, and then get something to eat."

So they had a plan.

On the drive to the hotel, Cassie opened up to them a little.

"I just couldn't do it," she repeated. "We've dated for so long I know everybody expected us to get married, but things haven't been what they should have been for some time."

"Is there someone else?" Jim asked, looking at his daughter intently through the rear-view mirror.

"Not really, but I shouldn't have had the thoughts I had when I bumped into Dan Harris a few weeks ago, and I think Rob might still be in love with Tanya Snyder," Cassie said. "It's all mixed up. It isn't the way it's supposed to be when you say 'I do.'"

"OK," was all Jim said in response.

"I'm glad we didn't put a down payment on that house," Cassie added.

"No kidding," her father agreed.

After dropping his wife and daughter off at the hotel, Jim returned home and packed an overnight bag for himself and Chris. He swung by the church too, where he retrieved Cassie's purse and car keys from an end table in the church parlor. Luckily the room wasn't locked and they were untouched. Her cell phone was beeping in her handbag though, and when he looked she had 37 messages.

When he got back to the hotel, both women were on lounge chairs next to the pool. Later that afternoon they went out to an early dinner, and then watched TV that evening back at the hotel.

It was almost noon the following day when the couple took Cassie back to her condo. When Jim pulled into the parking lot of the complex, they were appalled to see all the shrubbery around Cassie's building had been yanked out and tossed onto the front porch of her unit. The pile was so high that no one could get in the door. Even the small, ornamental cherry tree that had stood in the front lawn, looking like a perfect pink parasol, was uprooted.

Cassie and Jim got out of the car and Dave Wilson, the complex's maintenance manager, filled them in.

"It was your intended and his buddies," Dave told Cassie. "They came over here last night after they'd been drinking, and caused all this damage. They got on the front-end loader I'd rented to dig out that ditch next to the parking lot, and went crazy. I called the cops, and right now they're all sitting in the county jail."

"Oh my," Cassie said, her eyes wide.

"They're going to have to sit there for awhile, because Rob's parents went on your honeymoon last night, since that was non-refundable," he continued with the air of someone from a small town that knows everyone's business. "I'm waiting for the insurance adjuster to arrive to look at the damage, in case there is a problem getting Rob and his cohorts to pay," he added. "He's late, but after he's done looking at it, I'll carve a path to your door so you can get in."

"Thank you," was all Cassie said, still shocked by the destruction.

Jim and Cassie walked back to Jim's car, where Chris was still seated. "Do you think he'll try to do her harm?" Chris asked Jim after they told her what had happened.

"No; I think they were drunk and they were letting off steam," Jim replied. "Sitting in jail for awhile should do them good."

A few weeks later, Jim stopped into a local bar to have a beer after finishing a run with his truck and noticed Rob's father, Paul, at the far end of the bar. Jim had only met him twice — once at a restaurant when Cassie arranged a meeting of the parents, and once at the wedding rehearsal. He had a long beard and his hair looked like it hadn't been combed since the wedding.

Jim picked up his beer, covered the distance in a few steps, and sat on a bar stool beside Paul.

"Paul," he said, nodding. "I want to apologize for everything, but I guess it's better that they didn't get married than if they had to get a divorce down the road."

"Your daughter doesn't know a good thing when she has it," Paul said accusingly.

Jim didn't play. "It was a hell of a mess, wasn't it?" Jim said agreeably, and Paul nodded. "I guess it's a woman's prerogative to change her mind."

"I suppose," Paul agreed. "Her timing stunk. My son is all over her now though. And we think you should pay us back for the tuxes."

Jim didn't respond.

The two men sat in silence for a while, sipping their beer. Jim left a $10 bill on the bar a little later, said "See you" to Paul, and headed home, convinced his family had dodged a bullet.

7

Daughter's Day

"Now let me get this straight," Doreen said, folding her arms against her ample chest while tottering on 4-inch heels. "You're getting your mother jewelry and a card, you're taking her out to lunch, you're sending her flowers, and you don't even like her?"

"Yes. Tomorrow is Mother's Day," Cheryl replied, because to her those last four words explained everything.

"Wow," Doreen replied, sinking into a black vinyl loveseat in the rec room of the homeless shelter where she was staying. Cheryl had been a volunteer there for about four months, and the two had become friends. "What would you give her if she wasn't such a bitch?"

That's a good question. Cheryl ran her fingers through her short, black hair. It was all done from a sense of duty more than affection, because her mother had always been judgmental, critical, and non-supportive.

Her mother's mood swings and unpredictable rages were the

worst, but the family had almost grown accustomed to them over the years.

When Cheryl was a teenager, most of their fights had been over clothing, boys, the state of Cheryl's bedroom, and her supposed lack of work ethic. When her mother went into one of her rages, it was impossible for anyone to walk away. Cheryl had to remain quietly in the room where it occurred and wait until she was finished.

There was no pleasing her, and Cheryl got the worse of it as the oldest sibling.

Her mother was a professional ballerina before her marriage. Soon after she met and married Cheryl's father, however, she became pregnant with Cheryl. When she tried to return to the competitive world of dance after an extended maternity leave, it had moved on without her. She went to some auditions afterwards, but then gave up, and blamed the loss of her career on her motherhood.

Cheryl knew most of her friends had mothers who loved them unconditionally, which made her wistful and a little jealous. Cheryl always felt if she were to experience her mother's love she'd have to earn it, but no matter what she did it was never enough. It was like being a caged hamster spinning endlessly on a wheel, with no way out.

When Cheryl was 12, her father had insisted his wife see a therapist. She'd gone for a short period of time, but there had never been any improvement. Her mother had a supply of prescription medicines from her family doctor that were supposed to help, but she complained they made her sleepy, and quit taking them.

Now and then she had periods when she seemed to be better, but the family walked on eggshells around her due to her mood swings. It was like being in a minefield, with no clue where the bombs were or what would set them off.

Life got much better for Cheryl when she was finally old enough to move out. Her modest house on the outskirts of the next-biggest city had been a lifeline. She scheduled her short visits home only when necessary.

The strategy worked at first. Her mother seemed to try to be on her best behavior when Cheryl came home initially. But when she began menopause last winter, she was as bad as usual. The mood swings were back in full force. She said she couldn't sleep, she had hot flashes, and no medicine could cure her migraines. She complained constantly, and Cheryl was a main topic of her criticism.

For the last two years her most prevalent complaint about Cheryl centered on Cheryl's decision to break up with her boyfriend, Steve, an up-and-coming lawyer with political aspirations. Her mother believed she'd thrown away her best chance for happiness, but Cheryl knew it would never work shortly after their first date.

Money, status, and keeping up appearances were important to her mother. Cheryl had a responsible job, but she knew her mother would be dismayed to learn she'd been spending a great deal of time volunteering at the homeless shelter across town. She would consider it a waste of time instead of a contribution to society.

"Why do you put up with her?" Doreen was asking her now, tapping her long, magenta fingernails on a side table beside the love seat. No matter how little money Doreen had, she was never without colorful nail polish.

"She's my mother," Cheryl replied simply. "Honor thy father and mother, you know."

"You don't owe her anything; you didn't ask to be born," Doreen pointed out. "If she can't be nice, I wouldn't bother with her."

"She has problems," Cheryl answered quietly.

"Hmph," Doreen grunted in reply.

"Do you ever see your mother?" Cheryl asked, curious.

"Honey, I gave up on that junkie years ago," Doreen said resolutely. "I don't know where she is, and I don't care."

"She doesn't even know she has a grandchild?" Cheryl pressed.

"No. She didn't care about her kids. Why would she care about her grandkids?" Doreen asked.

Cheryl let it drop. Doreen had enough problems to tackle to get back on her feet.

The following morning before Cheryl started the two-hour trip to her hometown, she paused a moment with her coffee mug and stepped out of French doors onto her house's small rear deck. She set the mug onto the railing made of pressure-treated lumber, just like the deck, and took a deep breath.

Stretching ahead and a bit to the right, her lawn joined one of the fields belonging to an adjacent farm that had not yet succumbed to urban expansion. A rickety fence with an even more rickety gate marked the property line, but the tender green grass and the already abundant dandelions blooming among the blades of grass didn't acknowledge boundaries.

An old redbud tree with gnarly bark cast its branches above the fence and marked the presence of the gate. It wasn't in bloom yet. Cheryl hoped it was just late, and not dead. Other trees, just starting to bud, stretched out in a line on the right-hand side of the field, only to meet another tree line running horizontally about 100 yards ahead.

Birds chirped happily, and in the distance a church bell welcomed worshipers. Cheryl took another deep breath of the sweet air offered on this second Sunday in May, savored the smell of the fresh earth and grass, and willed herself to make it last in her memory throughout the day. It was a tranquil setting of a tender, unspoiled world offering fresh starts and infinite possibilities.

I wish I could stay here today Cheryl thought, but a couple of minutes later she turned, went back into the house, locked the back door, and set her half-empty mug in the kitchen sink. A few minutes later she picked up her purse and a small, pink gift bag she had placed on a chair in her living room the night before, went out the front door, and closed and locked it resolutely.

Cheryl played music on her car's audio system during the trip, and the time passed swiftly. Before long she was parking her blue hatchback in the parking lot of the restaurant where she'd agreed to meet her parents. Blue periwinkles peeked from the bases of the light poles dotting the parking lot, adding color to even the dull gray of the pavement.

Cheryl's younger sister and brother, along with his know-it-all wife, weren't going to be there. Her sister was conveniently on a business trip on the other side of the country. Her brother's family was visiting her sister-in-law's parents this afternoon, and would stop by her parents' house this evening.

"Hi Dad, Mom," Cheryl nodded when she met them in the restaurant's lobby. "Were you waiting long?"

"No, we just got here," her father answered.

Her mother turned her attention to the hostess, and informed her their party was complete, and she could take them to their table now. Then she reached into her bag, drew out a tissue, and sneezed. "My allergies are terrible," she said. "You'd think they'd spray or something to get rid of all this pollen in the air."

Cheryl gave her mother the gift bag after they were seated.

"You shouldn't have," her mother said, although they both knew Cheryl would have been chastised later behind her back if she hadn't supplied a gift.

"It's just something small," Cheryl said.

"The flowers you ordered from Niven's were plenty, especially on what little salary you make," her mother said. "Have you done anything recently about trying to find a new job?"

Cheryl liked her job. She counted to 10 and tried not to take it as an insult.

The gift bag contained a non-committal Mother's Day card and a small, square box filled with an expensive piece of costume jewelry.

"Thank you," Cheryl's mother said politely of the silver and gold herringbone necklace, but her tone made Cheryl wonder what was wrong with it. It was from a well-known jewelry manufacturer, and she bought it at a major department store. It hadn't been cheap.

"Really, it's nice," her mother added doubtfully, making things worse.

Cheryl picked up her menu and tried to push ahead.

"Everything is good here; what are you in the mood for?" she asked no one in particular as she looked over the menu.

"I'm thinking a steak," her father replied.

"The last steak I had here was overdone and I'm not in the mood for seafood, so I'm not sure," her mother said. "And where is our waitress? Service here has dropped off."

Well, you picked the place Cheryl thought, but left the thought unspoken.

Eventually a young waitress arrived and took their orders. Cheryl's father ordered his steak, her mother decided on the vegetable plate, and Cheryl chose shrimp with pasta.

The conversation went along fairly well until about halfway through the meal. Her parents had been discussing possible vacation spots, but then her mother turned her attention to Cheryl.

"Have you gained weight?" her mother asked her. "It looks like you have. Your complexion looks a little blotchy too. You should take better care of yourself.

"No wonder why you don't get asked out much," she continued. "I don't know why Steve wasn't good enough for you, but you blew that opportunity. You don't have many prospects, and you'll never find anyone now. You've made a mess of your life. You better get your act together soon; you aren't getting any younger."

Perhaps it was the harshness in her mother's voice, her conversation with Doreen playing in her subconscious, or the last straw, but Cheryl quietly exploded. She was sure her mother wouldn't make a scene in public, but that didn't mean she wouldn't. She picked up her plate, swore, silently asked for forgiveness from the Lord above, and dumped her remaining pasta over her mother's head.

"Cheryl!" her mother sputtered, her eyes glaring. Most of the pasta was in her lap, although a couple strands highlighted her silver hair. One noodle was plastered to her skin from her temple to below her clenched jaw.

"Cheryl!" her father declared, his eyes wide.

"I have had enough," Cheryl seethed. She didn't raise her voice, but she didn't have to because everyone in the general vicinity was watching and quiet as a rock. "Happy Mother's Day, Mother, and now leave me alone!" she hissed, rising from her chair.

It was so quiet the diners could hear the PA system, which was playing "Somewhere, Over the Rainbow" for ambiance.

"Why, whatever has gotten into you? Sit down! You're making a scene!" her mother answered in a shocked but hushed tone.

"Now, ladies," Cheryl's father started.

Cheryl cut him off. "Leave it, Dad," she said. "This is between Mom and me."

"I've never done anything to deserve your shit," Cheryl continued, glaring at her mother. "It's not my fault you had to give up dancing. That's too much guilt to pile on a baby, and I'm finally done taking the blame. I know I have to respect my elders. But right now, for once, I'm setting some limits. You don't have to love me, but I deserve respect too!"

Cheryl's father stared wide-eyed at his daughter.

The diners at the adjacent tables didn't know where to look, so most of them peered into their plates.

A young girl dressed in her Sunday best seated three tables over whispered "Mommy! Those ladies need a time out!" loud enough for everyone to hear.

Cheryl's mother stared at her oldest daughter, shocked.

"Well, I never," she sputtered and stood. Several strands of Cheryl's pasta clung to her blouse, while others slid onto the carpet. "You ruined Mother's Day!"

"Yes," Cheryl agreed.

"I can't say anything to you!" her mother continued.

"No, Mother, you can't if you're going to keep up the constant criticism," Cheryl told her earnestly. "You can't live your life through me. We're so different and you think I'm such a loser, I don't know why you would even want to try. You're my mother, and I will honor you because of that fact. But I will no longer put up with you constantly criticizing me for everything!"

The young waitress chose that moment to reappear. She took one look at the situation and rushed to find additional napkins.

"Well, I'm sorry you feel that way, Cheryl," her mother said coldly. "We will be leaving now."

The waitress returned with the napkins. "Would you like more spaghetti?" she asked cheerfully, and then when she came under the older woman's glare, she said, "Oh, I guess not."

"I'll wear this order out," Cheryl's mother said.

But the waitress had more instructions to follow. "No dessert then?" she asked with a smile, as her manager had emphasized she was to promote the dessert until they ran out of it. "We have a wonderful crumb topping on our special Mom's apple pie!"

"I think not," Cheryl's mother said. "We'll take our check and leave."

Cheryl said a quick goodbye to her father as her mother marched to their car without another word.

Driving home, even Cheryl couldn't believe she had finally stood up to her mother. Guilt washed over her, because she knew her mother had issues. She also knew she had broken a commandment, and she could have found a better way to handle it. But she was also relieved she'd finally let her mother know how she felt. She knew her relationship with her mother would continue to be a challenge, but for now a huge weight was off her shoulders.

The next move is yours, Mom Cheryl thought as she pulled into her driveway, dodging a small brown rabbit that darted across her path. *I will always try to help you, but I'm not going to let you walk all over me ever again.*

Since she'd finally said what she wanted to say, a new sense of optimism enveloped her. She would no longer be the victim. As she got out of her car and headed towards her little house, she had a new sense of self-worth and confidence, and a spring in her step. She felt free, similar to the buds unwrapping on branches everywhere on that glorious Mother's Day afternoon.

Two weeks later, while she was doing some spring-cleaning, her mother called while she was running the vacuum in her living room. Cheryl could tell she'd rehearsed her first few lines, but they were music to her ears because she never thought she'd hear them.

"Cheryl, I'm sorry I've been such a bad mother," she heard her mother say. "I love you, and I want to do better. I've been to a new therapist, and he feels certain he can help me."

"That's great, Mom; I love you too," Cheryl replied. "I'm sorry Mother's Day went badly."

"Maybe you could come over sometime soon, and we'll try again," her mother replied. "Only maybe we won't go out for pasta."

Cheryl giggled. They spoke a while longer about inconsequential things, and when they hung up the phone they both felt much better.

Happy Daughter's Day Cheryl said to herself as she went back to her cleaning.

8

Soul Food

"Hi, Mr. Hunley, are you going fishing?"

A lesser man would have responded with a sarcastic comment, considering he was wearing fishing apparel, holding a fishing pole, and standing on the bank of a stream. Rick Hunley simply smiled and said "Hi, Lucy, and yes I am" to his 8-year-old next-door neighbor.

Rick had been looking forward to Saturday all week. He intended to spend this whole glorious spring day drowning worms in the creek adjoining his small farm in Pennsylvania.

"Drowning worms" was what his brother Jeff called it. Jeff hadn't been much of an outdoorsman.

Rick liked to fish because it got him out in the fresh air and it gave him time to relax and think. This session was also his personal reward for getting his taxes done before the deadline. Lucy wasn't part of his ideal scenario, but more often than not she was exactly where she was now — nestled among the branches of an old silver maple tree beside the creek, her head buried in a book.

"What are you reading today, Lucy?" he asked.

"Nancy Drew," she said. "I read this one before, but I like it so much I'm reading it again."

"That's good," Rick replied. "It's important to be a good reader."

Rick took a few steps down the bank and laid his fishing equipment next to a big stump. After arranging the items to his liking, he took a worm out of an old blue coffee can, baited his hook, and made an expert cast out to an underwater hole where he knew both brown and rainbow trout congregated.

"I see you're fishing too," he said, nodding to Lucy's old fishing pole propped up beside a rock, right below her tree. A red and white bobber marked the spot in the water where her line extended. "What are you using for bait?"

"Bubble gum," she replied matter-of-factly.

"How are you going to land a fish when you're up a tree, reading?"

"Oh, I'm good at multi-tasking," Lucy assured him. "All women are."

Rick smiled.

"Buster and Percy like to fish too," Lucy told him, referring to his dogs. The two mutts had sniffed the area and they must have deemed it safe, since they were now stretched out on the bank, enjoying the sun that peeked through Lucy's tree and others nearby. Lucy's family took care of Rick's dogs for him when he had to travel, although that wasn't often.

The pair settled into an easy silence. Lucy flipped her pages intermittently, and pushed the nosepiece of her bright blue plastic glasses in closer on her round face every now and then. She was wearing jeans and a sweatshirt with a white, lilac, and pink unicorn on it, and she had white sneakers on her feet. Her long brown hair was in pigtails.

It was a little chilly beside the water, which was typical for late

April. Rick had jeans on too, and a red-plaid flannel shirt over a navy-blue T-shirt. He wore a tan vest, its pockets crammed with tackle and other supplies. He wore the same brown work boots he wore every day on his job as an electrician. A red-plaid cap that didn't match his shirt was on the top of his head. Although this was his land and he could have fished it for free, his fishing license was pinned to his cap.

There was a big, flat gray rock on the bank, and he sat on it while he held onto his pole. Then he placed the pole on the ground for a minute while he cut a Y-shaped stick off a bush, tore off its leaves, stuck it in the ground in front of him, and placed his rod on his impromptu stand.

Rick was glad the only people at his favorite fishing spot were himself and Lucy. On opening day the creek had been crammed with fishermen. They were attracted by the prime spot and the fact the creek was a stone's throw from the two-lane rural road that ran beside it for miles, so no hiking was needed to get to the creek. Rick could have posted "No Trespassing" signs on his section of shoreline but it would have been no use, and he wasn't one to hoard his little piece of Paradise.

Although it was only two weeks after opening day of trout season, the crowd had moved on to other activities or other fishing spots. It wouldn't surprise Rick if two or three other guys showed up later, but for now it was just Lucy and him.

The casual onlooker would have thought the scene was serene, but the creek was busy. Ripples of clear water danced around its rocks, and insects darted over the water's surface. Birds chirped from the brush alongside the creek. At one point a turtle that had been sunning itself on a log made a little splash as it slipped into the water.

The banks were full of green brush, saplings, and brown leaves left over from last fall. Rick knew there were plenty of deer in the area, but they were usually bedded down in the brush at this time of day.

Light green leaves were either waving from their branches or about to unfold. The sky was a brilliant light blue, and puffy, white clouds dotted the sky. Now and then a hawk flew overhead.

The smell of young grass and free-flowing water mingled with the rich aroma of the earth. Rick took several deep breaths, and willed himself to remember it always.

Gray rocks and bright-green grasses punctuated the banks. A big gray rock lay on the other side of the bank, right at the water's edge. Part of it was submerged. Rick knew trout would lie beside it to keep cool. Moss could be seen on this big rock and other smaller rocks in the water, while moss and other vegetation grew on the smaller rocks that were submerged or partially submerged.

Since the water was clear, stones could be seen on the floor of the creek, placed as perfectly as an installer would lay expensive tile in a mansion's master bathroom. Although the stones were gray, brown, black, tan, yellow or white, they all looked brown from above.

A female mallard duck and six ducklings waddled by on the bank on the other side of the creek. The mother duck pecked at stray bugs and then slipped into the water, turned, and encouraged her children to do the same. Five started their swimming lesson right away, while the sixth had to muster up some confidence before he, too, took the plunge.

Lucy noticed them too.

"Ducks!" she said, and Rick nodded. He picked up his pole and made another cast in a different spot.

He got his first nibble less than a minute later. Less than a minute after that a 9-inch brown trout was on his stringer, its chain wrapped around a sapling at the water's edge.

"Nice one!" Lucy said and went back to her book.

While he fished, Rick's thoughts drifted back to Dec. 18, when he'd lost his brother, Jeff, in a traffic accident. Another brother, Craig, had met the same fate several Decembers earlier. Their parents were elderly and still alive, but now Rick was down to one sibling, his sister, Kathy.

The family tragedies had been shocking. None of it made sense.

Rick's pole bent with another strike, and he pulled in a rather large perch. He was concentrating on trout today though, so after he pulled the hook out of its mouth he returned it to the water and watched it swim away.

As he continued to fish, thoughts crowded his brain as he contemplated the meaning of life and came to no satisfactory conclusions.

Lucy must have noticed he was deep in thought. "What are you thinking about, Mr. Hunley?"

"Oh, just things," Rick replied. "Fishing is good for the soul, you know."

"The soul or the sole?"

"What?" Rick answered, confused.

"You know, the soul like what goes to heaven when we die, or a fillet of sole, like a fish," she answered.

"Oh!" Rick said, smiling. "A soul like what goes to heaven."

"Oh, I thought it was a sole, since we're fishing," Lucy said without missing a beat.

"Those are homophones," she informed him less than a minute later.

"Homo what?"

"Homophones," she giggled. "We just talked about them at school. They are words that sound the same but are spelled differently and mean different things."

"Well, OK then," Rick said. "I'll take your word on that."

Another minute passed.

"You know, shoes have soles too," Rick pointed out.

Lucy giggled, and watched Rick land another trout. This one was a rainbow, and it was well over the 7-inch minimum size.

The afternoon continued on, and the number of fish on Rick's stringer continued to increase. When he had his daily limit of five, he called it quits. The dogs were getting restless, and it was time to think about dinner. The dogs would get their regular chow because of the bones, but Rick was looking forward to fresh trout for supper.

Suddenly Lucy's fishing pole bent and slipped off the rock it was resting on. Rick lunged for it and caught the base of it right before it went into the water. Whatever was dragging it was pretty big.

"I got one!" Lucy shrieked. She slammed her book shut, clambered down the tree, and was beside Rick in an instant.

"Here, you take it; it's your pole and your fish," Rick told her, handing her the pole. Whatever was on the end of it was putting up a fight. "Take the clicker off," Rick directed.

The fish darted and weaved as it tried everything to get free. "This is hard; he's really big!" Lucy said.

"You can do it; just keep with it and reel him in," Rick replied.

Lucy did as she was told. Rick had his net out ready to scoop up whatever was on the end of her line. It turned out to be a 19-inch-long catfish.

"He's a monster!" Rick told her. Lucy was so excited she clapped, and the dogs were so excited they barked.

"What are you going to do with him now?" Rick asked.

"Take my picture with him, and then set him free," Lucy said. "It's not time for him to go to heaven yet. I might want to catch him another time."

"OK then," Rick said. He produced his cell phone out of one of the pockets of his vest, snapped a picture of one big fish and one happy little girl, took the hook out of the fish's mouth, and let it drop back into the water. Smiling contentedly, together they watched it swim quickly away.

9

A Memorial Day Letter

Maria Ricardo looked at the hundreds of excited people filing into the grandstands of the Indianapolis Motor Speedway on the last Sunday morning in May. She'd been told the Indianapolis 500 was the largest single-day sporting event in the world, but right now, even though people surrounded her, all she felt was the crushing pain of loneliness and fear.

Attending the Indy 500 had always been on the bucket list of her youngest son, Seb. She wished with all her heart he was with her instead of being on a dangerous mission somewhere in Afghanistan with the U.S. Army.

It's not like I'm alone Maria chided herself, trying to beat back the debilitating fear that had plagued her after reading Seb's last e-mail. He'd said he might not be in touch for a while, but she wasn't to worry.

She hadn't stopped worrying since she read his instructions not to.

Maria had a large family. Her other children used to tease her that Seb was her favorite, but it had become such common knowledge somewhere along the line everyone just accepted it. She had an uncommon bond with him, which made the nightmare she'd been having about him lately even worse. She's woken up more than once during the last two weeks with her heart beating wildly as she saw her baby being blown to pieces by a bomb in her dreams.

Seb's second tour of duty was about up, and he was weighing the pros and cons of re-enlisting.

Maria knew exactly what she wanted him to do. Yesterday she'd written him a heartfelt letter to try to convince him to rejoin civilian life. It was still in her pocketbook, stamped but not yet mailed. There was no mail pick-up until Tuesday, anyway.

Maria had won tickets to attend this year's Indy 500 in a raffle at work. She wasn't a race fan and knew little about the sport. Seb followed it, so she thought she'd go and have something interesting to tell him in her next letter, or when they spoke via Skype. She was relatively new to Indianapolis too, and it seemed everyone at the hotel where she worked had been to the race at least once and followed it every year. She figured she might as well see what it was all about.

The raffle prize was two race tickets, so she was there with her daughter-in-law, Sophia. Juan, who was Sophia's husband and another one of Maria's sons, had dropped the women off a few streets away early in the morning and they'd simply followed the crowd. By a stroke of luck when they decided to ask directions to their seats, they weren't far away. Now, safely in their metal seats in a huge, covered grandstand flanking the frontstretch several hours before the start of the race, they were people watching.

Maria picked up her souvenir program and riffled through its pages. She absent-mindedly landed on a page with quick facts about the Indianapolis Motor Speedway. She was surprised to learn that Vatican City, the Taj Mahal, Yankee Stadium, the White House,

Liberty Island, the Roman Coliseum, Rose Bowl Stadium, and Churchill Downs could all fit inside the 2.5-mile oval that lay in front of her, with room to spare.

"Excuse me, are you Seat 3?" asked a pleasant-looking woman a little younger than Maria. "I think we're right beside you," she said, motioning to an equally pleasant-looking man beside her.

"Yes; we're in three and four," Maria confirmed with a nod to Sophia.

After the couple got settled, the lady offered her hand to Maria and introduced herself.

"I'm Barbara Allen; my nephew is Travis Allen."

"Very pleased to meet you," said Maria, mystified. "Who is your nephew?"

"Travis Allen, Number 4," Barbara replied, not unkindly.

"Oh! Is he a driver? I'm sorry; this is my first race. I don't know much about racing," Maria admitted.

"Oh! How wonderful you came then!" said Barbara, not missing a beat. "We'll be glad to answer any questions you have; we've been going to this race for most of our lives."

"Gracias," Maria said, slipping back to her native Spanish. "Tell me about your nephew; I will cheer for him too," she said. "And do you have any children yourself?"

"We don't have any children, but we're so close to Travis he could be ours," Barbara said. "We're his godparents."

"Travis is 24, and this is his second Indy 500," she continued. "He started racing go-karts when he was 5, and he won a lot of championships in them. Then he moved into formula cars. He struggled for a while until he got with a better team, and he won two championships in them too. He didn't raise enough money to do a whole season of IndyCar last year, but he was in the 500 and two other races.

He didn't do well here last year, but it wasn't his fault; his car had an electrical problem about three-fourths of the way through the race. So, now he's here to try again!"

"My," Maria said. "He has to raise the money to race?"

"Oh yes; it's like that for almost all the drivers," Barbara said. "It's so expensive."

"I see," Maria said before the announcer and a college band marching by them on the frontstretch drowned the rest of her sentence out.

"We were in the garage area to wish him well earlier, and we'll see him after the race, but there were so many people over there we came to our seats early," Barbara added a little later. "The pre-race festivities are always special before the Indy 500. The whole day honors the military."

"It does?" Maria asked. She knew this was Memorial Day weekend, but she didn't know anything about the pre-race festivities.

"Yes," Barbara confirmed. Then, seeing the tiny American flag pin on Maria's blouse, she asked if there was anyone in Maria's family who was in the service.

"Yes, my youngest son, Seb, is on a dangerous mission in Afghanistan right now," Maria confided. "He told me not to worry, but I can't help it."

"I understand," Barbara said. "I worry about Travis racing at such high speeds, but he doesn't have anyone shooting at him, and we see him often."

Maria gave her a small smile. "It is similar," she said. "I'm hoping he'll not sign back up when his stint is over in July."

"I understand," Barbara repeated. "But you keep watching; I think you'll enjoy the pre-race festivities."

Several antique race cars were on the track in front of them now, driven by retired race car drivers who everyone seemed to know except for Maria and Sophia. More bands followed, and the announcers told the crowd about each group as it went by.

With all the action in front of her and the comforting conversation with her new friend, Maria started to feel better. During small lulls in the parade, Maria asked Barbara other questions about the race, and Travis in particular.

"There's his car!" Barbara said a few moments later. "They put it in the pits first, and tow it out onto the track for the start."

"The cars are smaller than they look on TV," Maria said.

"Yes; they're designed for speed," Barbara agreed.

As more people filed into the grandstands, there was a definite buzz in the air as the excitement built. A large scoring pylon flashed all sorts of messages and displays. Maria noticed many people seemed to have come with family or friends. For most it seemed to be an annual excursion.

She marveled at all the people wearing clothing advertising individual drivers, turning themselves into walking billboards. Maria spent several minutes watching a man wearing an outfit done in a black-and-white checkered print. He looked like a clown to Maria, but other fans greeted him warmly, and he enjoyed the attention.

Soon the 33 race cars were pushed onto the frontstretch in the order of their starting positions. There would only be one winner, but they all looked capable to Maria.

Since she was short, she had to stretch on her toes to see everything, but she also noticed a long line of trucks making their way from Turn 4 to the pit area.

"The track does a nice job of honoring our service people every year," Barbara told her.

That's when Maria realized there were service people from all branches of the military standing in the bed of each truck, and they were getting a standing ovation as they went by the crowds.

"There are men from the Army, just like Seb," Maria said, swallowing hard as she saw their smiling faces, so young, confident, and proud.

The trucks had made a complete lap of the track, and all the while the soldiers received standing ovations.

"You must be so proud of your son," Barbara said.

"Yes; proud, but afraid for him, too," Maria admitted.

"I'm often afraid for Travis too, but racing is his passion, and he wants so much to do it," Barbara said. "All we can do is support them, and hope for the best."

"Yes," Maria said quietly.

Later, after the drivers were introduced, prayers were offered, and "Taps," "America the Beautiful," "The Star-Spangled Banner," and "Back Home Again in Indiana" were performed, the command was given to the drivers to start their engines. As the engines revved up, Maria reached into her pocketbook and pulled out the letter she had written but not yet mailed.

I'll write another letter, and tell him I'll try to support him regardless of his decision she told herself. *I can't ask him to be someone less than who he is.*

She'd drop it into a big mailing envelope so she could include her Indy 500 souvenir program too. She would tell him all about the race, and about meeting Travis's godparents.

And maybe next year, we can all come to this race together she prayed as she tore her first letter into pieces and threw them in the air, to be caught in the same Hoosier breeze that lifted hundreds of balloons skyward as the field headed towards Turn 1.

10

Puzzle Pieces

Michelle attached her autism ribbon lapel pin to Bear's red halter as he stood patiently on cross ties in the aisle next to the stalls of the therapeutic riding center. She was grooming the registered Morgan for the center's horse show in its indoor riding arena later that April morning and early afternoon.

April was national autism awareness month, and all the volunteers like Michelle received a free pin as a thank you for their service. It depicted a colorful ribbon of interlocking puzzle pieces. Its design was appropriate, as the families Michelle saw at the center were caught in a never-ending puzzle as they tried to connect with their autistic relatives.

Michelle had been volunteering at the center at least twice a month for several years, and she'd seen first hand the results the therapists were making with the special children they served. A horse owner herself, she'd been attracted to the program as a way of using her love of everything equine to make a difference in the lives of these children with special needs.

It was a pleasant, short drive to get there from her home, and the grounds of the riding center were always beautiful. Right now the pastures were full of delicate green grass too fresh for the herd to be out on long for fear of colic. Redbud trees and forsythia were in bloom, and the magnolia trees and lilac bushes were in bud. A delicate breeze had greeted Michelle when she walked to the barn from the parking lot. The sky was a light blue and streaked with thin, white water vapor too delicate to form into clouds.

The center adjoined a botanical garden, and the garden's volunteers made sure the entrance to the riding center was always beautiful. White, yellow, and purple crocuses shivered in the breeze from their places in large gray containers flanking the entrance. Phlox in the colors of lilac, a deeper purple, and magenta covered the ground to the right of the doors, serving as a dazzling base for red and lavender azaleas which would unfold as soon as the weather got a little warmer. A pussywillow tree already showed its grayish fur, while beside it stood a snowball bush laden with green balls that would soon turn white.

After Michelle finished cleaning Bear's feet with her hoof pick, Bear yawned and looked at her with his wise, liquid-brown eyes. He was a retired trail horse who was on loan to the center from his owner, who lived in Indiana. He was Michelle's favorite horse on the farm. Pure black, he was perfect for the duty due to his calm demeanor, patience, and sure-footed gaits.

Michelle's assignment was to groom him before his classes, and to lead him around the indoor riding arena during the sessions. Two other people would walk beside Bear on either side as a safety measure in case his rider would need help. Her partners today in that effort would be Joan, a woman slightly older than herself whom Michelle didn't know well, and Bill, a college student who had just started volunteering there. Like Michelle, both had gone through a training course before they were permitted to help.

Rosemary, a physical therapist who put each rider through special exercises while they were mounted, would be their leader today. The purpose of the exercises was to improve each child's strength, balance, posture, flexibility, circulation, coordination, and breathing.

Today's session was similar to every session, except there was a larger audience than usual in the viewing stand because today's program was advertised as a special horse show. Many members of the riders' families had shown up in support. There were two TV crews on site too, and at least three print reporters were asking questions and taking notes.

Bear's rider for this session would be Tommy, a 5-year-old boy they'd been working with for almost a year. He'd come a long way from his first session, when he threw a temper tantrum at the first sight of a horse. His attention span was longer now, and he did most of the exercises much easier. The sidewalkers still had to watch him carefully, however, because sometimes he kicked the horse under him for no reason, and sometimes he flailed his arms so vigorously he was in danger of falling off.

Rosemary had requested no saddle today. She thought riding bareback was helping Tommy to get a sense of where his own body was in relationship to Bear's.

Michelle gave her own medium-length brown hair a quick pass with Bear's body brush, unsnapped the cross ties, and led Bear towards the riding arena. Bear's gleaming if slightly stooped back was ready for Tommy to climb aboard with the help of a mounting block. Joan and Bill were already in position near the dark-green plastic steps, ready to help.

Tommy had been born prematurely to older parents, who were

both in attendance and supportive. He had an older brother and an older sister who were not autistic. The sister was with her parents in the viewing area, but the brother hadn't been able to make it to the show due to high school baseball practice.

"Have a good ride, Tommy!" his mother told him as Joan walked over and took his hand. None of them were surprised when Tommy didn't respond or even look at any of them. He was wearing the required riding helmet and staring at the ground through his large brown glasses, but the women could tell he was excited because he was flapping his right arm. His left arm was touching each of the buttons on his jeans jacket, in order, which was one of his habits when he was trying to contain his excitement.

"He didn't sleep well last night, so let's hope for the best," Tommy's mother told Rosemary.

Tommy was still looking at the dirt of the riding arena when he suddenly said "Bear!" Everyone within earshot smiled. Tommy rarely spoke, but his connection with Bear had opened up his verbal capacity. It had been the first word he ever spoke, in fact. Michelle knew many people with autism seldom speak, so Tommy's single word was a big accomplishment.

"Yes! This is your good friend, Bear!" Rosemary said, pleased. "And here are your other friends, Michelle, Joan, and Bill, to help us." Tommy didn't say a word in response, and was still looking at the ground.

Tommy's legs were slightly buckled, which caused him to have a permanent limp. Together, Joan and Bill helped Tommy step onto the mounting block, and then they helped him onto Bear's back. Michelle stood at Bear's head, holding his halter. Bear understood what was needed, and didn't move an inch.

"Grab onto Bear's mane, Tommy," Rosemary instructed him.

Tommy didn't comply, but after Bill gently pushed Tommy's fingers around strands of Bear's long, black mane, Tommy held on.

"Tommy! Are you ready to go?" Rosemary asked him, but Tommy didn't respond. He wasn't smiling, but he didn't seem to be unhappy, either. His eyes were focused on the autism awareness pin on Bear's halter. Tommy liked everything to be the same as it always was, and even this slight change rocked his routine.

"Can you tell Bear to walk on?" Rosemary asked Tommy.

He didn't respond verbally, but he slowly rocked his body in anticipation of Bear's easy gait.

Michelle gently pulled on the lead line, said "Walk" to Bear, and they started off. The sight of one boy on board a horse surrounded by four adults looked rather like a clipper ship leaving port, or a wagon train headed west.

"Sit up straight, Tommy!" Rosemary warned. "We need you to sit up straight and tall."

Tommy didn't pay any attention at first, like he hadn't even heard her, but about 30 seconds later he sat up straight and put his right hand high into the air, which was customarily his first exercise.

"Excellent, Tommy!" Rosemary said, but there was no response either way from Tommy.

The other riders in Tommy's class mounted or were lifted onto their horses' backs too. Eventually there were six horse-and-rider-and-helpers combinations walking in a circle around the large arena.

As they made their way, Rosemary asked Tommy to put his body into various positions. Each time, after a pause as if he was considering all the possibilities, he complied. After having him raise both hands over his head, one at a time, she had him touch each of his legs, his stomach, and his helmet. As Bear moved along at a walk, it pushed

Tommy's pelvis into motion, stimulating other bones, ligaments, and joints.

Rosemary gave Tommy's parents a smile as they walked by the viewing area. They beamed back.

"Good job, Tommy!" his father called out. "Sit up straight!"

The riders did different exercises while making five circles of the arena in all.

Rosemary could tell Tommy was close to his limit physically and mentally. He was increasingly looking at the large overhead lights of the arena, which put out a steady hum.

"Let's head over to the mounting block, and call it a session," she told Michelle. "He did well today! I think the audience helped!"

Both Tommy and Bear knew the routine when the session was over. After he was back on earth, Tommy clomped over to a waiting volunteer who had a plastic pan filled with broken pieces of carrots. Tommy took the pan from her, clomped back to Bear, and thrust it in front of him.

Bear fingered the first piece of carrot with his lips, and soon the aroma of carrot juice mingled with the pungent smell of the pine shavings and dirt floor of the arena combined with the heady smell of the animals themselves.

Tommy held onto the pan until Bear ate the last piece of carrot.

"Tell Bear 'Thank you!'" Rosemary instructed, but Tommy remained silent.

An announcer came on the arena's PA system.

"We have something special for you today," the announcer said. "Since this was a horse show for autism awareness, all of the students and all of the horses will get ribbons because they all did their best!"

The therapists, horse walkers and sidewalkers maneuvered their riders and horses into one long line in the center of the arena. Mr.

Martin, the facility's director, pinned a silk ribbon on each horse's halter, and handed each rider a similar ribbon.

Tommy and Bear each got a red one, which looked terrific against Bear's black hair. Tommy would get to take his ribbon home, while Bear's would be on display at the front of his stall, even though he spent most of his time in the paddocks or pastures.

"Now, can you all stand in a line for a photo?" the PA announcer asked, right before Whitney Houston's stirring rendition of "One Moment in Time" blasted over the speaker system.

After some pointing and maneuvering, all six riders stood in a line beside their mounts, but Tommy got mixed up. He stood next to Bear, but he was facing the wrong way as the photographer snapped the photo and the crowd in the viewing area clapped.

The photographer didn't miss a beat, however. After taking the first shot, with all the riders but Tommy looking at him, he darted to the opposite side of the line and took a photo of Tommy proudly holding his red ribbon. The backs of five other riders and the rumps of six horses flanked a smiling boy who was holding his bright red ribbon up, as if on cue.

Tommy's parents had the photo enlarged as large as possible, and hung it over the fireplace in the family's living room, where it became a treasured family heirloom.

11

The Orient Express March

"I'm sorry, Mr. Thompson, but there is no other seat available."

"If something should develop, please let me know," Brent Thompson told the airline ticket counter agent as he put his frequent-flyer card back in his wallet and then ran a hand through his thick brown hair. He flew overseas often, but usually in business or first class. Today, thanks to a rare mistake made by his own office staff, he was facing a 13-hour, 40-minute flight from Beijing, China to Newark, New Jersey sitting in the middle seat in the last row of the economy seats, right next to the restroom.

A highly regarded young architect, he was in Beijing overseeing plans for a new office building his firm was building there.

It had been a 70-minute ride to the airport from the hotel where he'd been staying. The ride should have taken 20 minutes, but a traffic jam and an inexperienced cabbie caused the delay. There must have been something wrong with the cab's cooling system too, because the cabbie stopped to add water to the radiator before he dropped him off at the Beijing airport a little before 2 p.m. for a 5 p.m. flight.

Brent stood in line for 45 minutes before he even reached the ticket counter. When it was finally his turn, he contemplated all his options with the agent for at least 30 minutes.

His ultimate destination was his home in Melbourne, Florida. He wanted to avoid a layover in Newark, New Jersey because the weather reports were predicting a spring snowstorm for the entire Northeast. It had been a mild winter, but Mother Nature was proving she still had the upper hand with this storm, which was rare for the third week of March. Although many would have welcomed the same storm at Christmas, no one wanted snow in spring.

Unfortunately all the flights from Beijing to San Francisco were booked solid. Brent's only alternative was to take his chances and go through New Jersey. After a three-hour, 20-minute layover there, he'd have a two-hour, 49-minute flight to Orlando, arriving in Florida at 12:49 a.m. local time tomorrow. After he got his luggage, he'd have another hour-and-a-half drive before he finally got home to his wife, Liz; his 9-year-old son, Matthew, and his 6-year-old daughter, Jessica.

This is starting to feel like the trip from hell, but I'm going to remain calm he vowed. *But I'm going through all this to attend an elementary school band concert?*

It was true. Since he worked overseas so much, Brent missed most of his children's school performances and activities. There was only a small window of opportunity for a trip home between the time he submitted his drawings for the new building to the client and the time he'd have to be back in China to make any necessary changes, secure the proper permits, and break ground on the new building. It was, for all intents and purposes, now or never if he wanted to attend Matt's last concert of this school year and hear his son's first solo.

So, with a resolute shake of his head, Brent headed to the security checkpoint. Since he traveled often he had a pass to use the shortest line, but he couldn't help but see an overweight woman crawling around one of the conveyor belts looking for a lost ring. She didn't know she didn't have to remove it to go through security.

At the end of another line, Brent noticed a man arguing with one of the workers who had confiscated a large bottle of vodka from his carry-on bag. Another man didn't argue but still looked upset when he wasn't allowed to bring a potent-looking corkscrew through the checkpoint. A younger man gave up a lighter he'd forgotten was in one of the pockets of his cargo pants. Meanwhile, a young woman with different colors of neon streaks in her hair bristled with impatience, finally stomping away on her thigh-high, black vinyl boots.

Brent proceeded to the boarding area, determined to make the best of it. The gate was packed, and many people, including Brent, were forced to stand. Brent and another man exchanged glances over a man about their age who not only had a seat for himself, but one for his carry-on bag and a third for his travel pillow and fast food.

Brent finally found a seat. It was empty because it was next to a teenage boy who was listening to loud rap music without headphones. Brent wished he could have charged his laptop and phone at one of the outlets, but someone had commandeered the plugs closest to him. It turned out to be a teenage girl who was minus a power strip and good manners.

The terminal's heat was off and it was cold to the point many people were shivering. Brent was glad he had a couple of layers of clothing on, as he was wearing a maroon polo shirt under an olive-green fleece vest. Khaki pants and loafers completed his travel garb. His expensive Rolex watch and his wedding ring were his only jewelry.

A few seats away a man was talking loudly on his cell phone and giving an endless, play-by-play account of a party he'd attended the previous night. There had been a buffet line with delicacies he was unfamiliar with, and his description of the food was making everyone around him a little queasy.

When Brent's section was called to board the Boeing 777, he showed his passport and boarding pass, and began the trek to the back of the plane of a completely full flight. His seat was the middle one in a group of three, in front of a restroom. The row consisted of nine seats in all. He passed several flight attendants as he made his way to the back of the plane. All seemed tired. None were particularly friendly or welcoming.

Eventually an elderly Asian man wearing baggy sweats crawled over him to take the window seat to his right. He was barefoot, and smelled like a combination of body odor and dead fish.

An overweight but pleasant American woman ended up at his left, on the aisle. In front of them was a woman with a red and runny nose who was traveling with three children under the age of 6, including a screaming infant. Brent felt sorry for her, but wished she'd cover her mouth when she sneezed.

Brent put on his noise-cancelling headphones and tried to get comfortable, which was impossible. He was thin, and he felt sorry for the woman to his left, who was holding her right arm as tight to her body as possible so as not to encroach on his space. With a seat only 17 inches wide she wasn't having much luck, and Brent knew no one could hold that position for over 13 hours.

The man on his right was ripe. Brent remembered he had a tiny jar of menthol ointment in his briefcase. He excused himself and rose to get it. When he found it, he dabbed a bit under his nose so he would smell it for a while and not his seatmate.

Finally everyone was seated and the plane left the gate, taxied down the runway, and lifted off for its long flight about 20 minutes late.

Brent started the flight by using his headphones to listen to the recordings he kept on his phone. That went well until the Internet feed started working intermittently and it became impossible to listen to the music, but at least he'd killed an hour and a half. The passengers who'd been watching a Chinese film on the small screens in front of each seat gave up unhappily too.

Due to past experience Brent thought the main meal for the flight would be served before its halfway point, so he decided to try to sleep awhile. The mother in front of him, her baby, and both of her older children had finally drifted off, so at least it was quieter. Two people were in line for the restroom. They were quiet, but their simple hovering over his row made Brent feel like even more of his personal space had disappeared.

He must have drifted off to sleep though, because two hours later he awoke to find the arms of both of his sleeping seatmates sprawled over him. He lifted them off him, crawled over the woman, and got in line for the restroom himself. When it was his turn he discovered the lock was broken, so one had to keep a foot or a hand on the door at all times.

The woman on the aisle was awake when he returned, and they chitchatted a bit. She was an English teacher going home for vacation. She showed him photos of her Scottish terrier, and he showed her photos of Liz and the kids. She admitted her fear of flying, and Brent tried to reassure her it was a generally safe if not always comfortable way to travel. While they talked they discovered an electrical plug in her armrest, and they took turns charging their phones.

Finally the flight attendants served the main meal. Brent knew not to expect much, but the limp salad, rubberized chicken, and something he thought was mashed potatoes were below even his lowest expectations. He was glad he had a couple of granola bars in his pockets. He shared them with the woman beside him, while the man in the window seat devoured his meal.

After the trays had been removed and the lines to the restroom got longer, the turbulence hit. The plane shook and dropped at least a foot. Several people, including the woman beside him, screamed, and everyone grabbed the back of the seat in front of them. One flight attendant tried to make her way down the aisle but fell, and decided to stay on the floor as the crew in the cockpit tried several different altitudes searching for quieter air.

It was a full 40 minutes later before the turbulence smoothed out, and by then everyone's nerves were shot.

Two college-age men Brent had seen drinking in the boarding area before departure got loud as they laughed and joked in Chinese. Brent knew enough of the language to recognize some crude phrases. Two flight attendants spoke to the men to ask them to keep it down. The flight attendants were teased instead, but eventually the men relented, drifted off to sleep, and quiet once again prevailed.

Brent read a book of short stories at that point. He'd never heard of the author, but "Twelve Stories for Spring" was a quick read. He noticed it was part of a four-part series, and he made a mental note to order the other three the next time he was online. It had been a good way to knock off more time until another meal was served.

This time the offering was a cup of noodles. He took one look at it and declined.

A little later the Internet came back up, which was a God's send. He spent the rest of the flight, including the extra 30 minutes they spent circling Newark Airport waiting their turn to land in the snowstorm, listening to his music and trying to stay calm.

Finally they made a bumpy landing. After another 25-minute delay on the tarmac waiting for an open gate, they finally pulled up next to a jetway. It was another 20 minutes before the last row of passengers could depart and head to customs.

Brent had a pass on his phone that made his entry through customs go smoothly, except his phone's screen kept locking up.

The customs agent was civil about it. "It's because so many people are using the system due to the storm," he explained. Finally it came up, Brent's passport was stamped, and he was on his way to another boarding area and another over three-hour wait.

When he arrived at that gate, however, he got bad news. All outgoing flights were now canceled due to the storm, which was much worse than predicted. He was being put up in an area hotel for the night until his flight to Orlando could try again in the morning.

"I'm stuck in Newark overnight, and I'm going to miss Matt's concert," he told Liz when his call went through. "Please tell him I'm sorry, but there isn't anything I can do about it. I tried."

The couple talked more, but Brent had to cut it short so he wouldn't miss the shuttle to the hotel. Since his luggage was going to remain in the airline's control he didn't have a change of clothes, but the airline did provide a small, plastic pouch filled with samples of toiletries. He shivered from the cold as he waited in line for the shuttle under the terminal's large roof, which overhung the sidewalk.

Brent knew he'd get no sleep in the hotel, but he thought it would help to at least stretch out on a bed. He hoped for the best, but didn't get it when the shuttle pulled up to a non-chain hotel near the airport. It was a mom-and-pop place, except even mom and pop had thrown in the towel long ago. The most polite term for it was seedy, although a few crocuses and grape hyacinths planted in two cement urns at the entrance did provide a touch of color as they peeked out through the snow.

While he waited in line with his fellow passengers, Brent dialed every major hotel chain he could think of in search of a room in Newark, but they were all booked due to the storm.

Brent's choices were either this place or back to the airport to try to sleep in a chair.

Brent wasn't sure if the man who signed them all in was an Indian or a Pakistani, but the procedure took a long time. Brent finally received a room key and headed outside to find his assignment, since the hotel had no interior hallways.

His room was in need of a gut job, but Brent knew it would have to do. He pulled down the thin bedspread and sheets of the full-size bed and looked for bed bugs. He didn't find any evidence of them, so he lay on the bed in the chilly room.

Sleep didn't come, however, because a couple in the adjoining room had found a different way to stay warm. Brent tried to ignore the constant, rhythmic thumping of the headboard against the thin wall their rooms shared, but it was no use.

I don't see how they both don't have a headache he thought. *I know I do.*

He was also cold.

I probably was so tired I didn't turn the heat on he thought, but when he got up and turned the dial on the wall, the heat didn't kick on. None of the lamps worked either. He opened the curtains over his solitary window to let in the glow from a streetlight. There were no headlights on the normally busy highway, which was now devoid of traffic due to the storm.

The last straw came when he used the tiny bathroom and discovered he had four thin washcloths but no towels.

He retraced his steps outside to the darkened lobby, hurrying due to the cold while trying not to fall in the snow.

The same clerk he'd met earlier knew what he was going to say before he said it.

"No electricity," he said. "We're trying to hook up the generator."

When Brent asked him to provide towels, suddenly the man did not understand English.

"No understand," he said. Brent knew without a doubt his lack of knowledge was a ruse, as the man had been reading the classifieds in "The Star Ledger" when he approached him, and his English had been fine earlier. Brent's face burned but he kept his temper in check. He counted to 10 and tried again.

"I know you understand," he said evenly. "I need towels. There are none in my room."

The man shook his head and looked at the floor.

Brent's best guess was either the hotel didn't have enough towels when it was at capacity, or his towels were among the piles waiting to be washed in the hotel's laundry room.

There was nothing else he could do but make his way back to his frigid room, wrap the thin bedspread around him, and wait for daybreak.

He took a quick, ice-cold shower, and dried off the best he could with the washcloths. Luckily he had a spare pair of boxers in his briefcase for such an emergency, and he was able to brush his teeth with the tiny toothbrush and even smaller tube of toothpaste the airline had provided. He put on the same set of clothes he'd worn yesterday and called a cab for the airport, as he wasn't about to wait for another shuttle.

The cab to the airport arrived 20 minutes later, which was a miracle considering the state of the roads. Plows had been out all night, but it was still snowing. The cab at least had heat.

When he arrived at the airport there was already a line at the ticket counter, so Brent got in line too. The scuttlebutt in line was the airport was still open and the runways were plowed, but all flights were either delayed or canceled.

Eventually he reached one of only two ticket agents who were working the counter.

"I don't have anything going to Orlando right now, but in two hours I think I can get you on a flight to Tampa," the agent told him.

"I'll take it," Brent said.

The two hours stretched to four hours, but Brent was able to get a cup of coffee and a cinnamon bun from one of the few open kiosks. He was relieved he had a seat on a flight, and it eventually took off. Of course his luggage didn't arrive in Tampa with him.

He stood in another line and inquired about a flight to Melbourne, but when he learned he could get there faster by car, he hiked to the rental car counters and rented a car.

After a stop at a diner for a hamburger and a large side of fries, he began the three-hour drive home.

It was the wee hours of the morning when he pushed the security pad for the garage door opener and let himself into his garage. By entering another code on another security pad mounted outside a steel door leading from the garage to the kitchen, he was finally home.

He craved a hot shower, so he took one and then crawled into bed with Liz.

"Hi, Honey," he said as he gave her a kiss. "How was the concert?"

"I'm glad you're home," she answered, hugging him back. "Matt did fine."

They fell asleep in each other's arms. Liz got up in the morning as usual, but Brent stayed in bed until noon.

When he finally rejoined his family, they were in the screened-in patio having a late brunch of pancakes, bacon, and freshly squeezed Florida orange juice.

"I'm sorry I missed your concert, Tiger," Brent said to Matt, ruffling his hair. "And Jess, how are you and Ginger today?"

"Fine, Daddy," Jess answered, clutching Ginger, a stuffed toy reindeer that was rarely out of her sight.

"I hear your solo went well," Brent added to Matt.

"It was OK," Matt mumbled back. "How long are you home this time?"

"Just a couple days," Brent said. "Do you think I could get a repeat performance later this afternoon?"

"I don't know," Matt said.

Brent left it at that for now, and got caught up on more family news as they ate. He and Liz would return his rental car to the Melbourne Airport later; right now he just wanted to be with his family.

After brunch, Brent excused himself and headed upstairs. He pulled down a tiny set of stairs in the hall ceiling, climbed into the attic, and looked around with a flashlight they kept by the attic entrance. About 10 minutes later he emerged with a small, dusty suitcase. He brought it to the kitchen, wiped it off, and placed it on the countertop.

"How about that concert, Matt?" Brent asked his son a few minutes later.

Matt looked up from a video game.

"Do I have to?" he asked his mom.

"It would be nice," Liz answered. "Your father went through a lot to get here for your concert. No one can control the weather, you know."

Matt reluctantly got his trumpet, set up his silver chrome music rack in the family room, and went through a couple scales to warm up. He played the whole piece that contained his solo, which included counting out nearly 30 seconds where the trumpet section rested. That was a relief to Mittens, the family cat, who disappeared under the couch at the first sign of the trumpet.

The family listened attentively. At first they weren't sure when the piece concluded, but when Matt gave a little flourish in the air with the bell of his trumpet and drew it away from his lips, they clapped.

"Do you think I could join you in a number?" Brent asked his son.

"Do you play?" Matt responded, confused. "You have a horn?"

Brent went into the kitchen, snapped open the latches of the case, and picked up a trumpet he hadn't played since college band.

"I didn't know you played the trumpet!" Matt said, surprised.

"I did a long time ago," Brent conceded. He put his lips to the mouthpiece and played a few notes, tentatively at first, and then with more confidence.

"Play a duet!" Liz suggested.

"It will have to be something basic; it's been a long time," Brent told Matt.

Matt fumbled through his music books, selected one, and turned to "Three Blind Mice."

They ran through it once, and everyone was laughing when they finished.

"Dad, don't go back and fix something when you make a mistake," Matt told him.

"OK," Brent agreed, laughing at himself.

They were much better the second time around. They played four more songs before finishing with an easy arrangement of "The Stars and Stripes March" and Brent conceded his lips were shot.

"That was fun!" Matt said.

Liz looked lovingly at her husband. Brent smiled at his family, and thought to himself they made the long trip home worth it.

12

Special Gifts

Still wearing her teal warm-up suit from her Zumba class that morning, Liz Thompson picked up the fourth and final 6-year-old girl in her black Porsche Cayenne and headed towards Piney Acres, a retirement home across town. Her church's kids' choir was performing for the residents there this afternoon, and it was Liz's turn to car-pool the children living on their side of Melbourne, Florida.

Liz's daughter, Jessica, was reluctant at best about the opportunity. She'd been chosen to accompany her fellow choir members on the piano for their rendition of "Jesus Loves Me." It would be her first public performance as a pianist.

The entire show would take about 30 minutes, and then the children would serve Girl Scout cookies and fruit punch to the residents. Liz was knee-deep in spring cleaning, and she hoped to straighten up the garage if she got back home in time.

At the moment on this bright Saturday afternoon in May, however, the four little girls in her care were deep in conversation on a variety of topics ranging from boys that were jerks, the best fast-food chicken nuggets, to teachers who called them by the wrong names. Jessica was quick to put her 9-year-old brother, Matt, in the former category.

At the steering wheel, Liz was trying to remember if she'd included everything on the list of paperwork she'd left for her assistant to handle before their closing on Monday. A real estate agent, Liz had recently sold a fixer-upper to a young couple with a toddler. They were first-time buyers with marginal financing, and they were relocating from New Jersey with no family in the area. She hoped she'd thought of everything, and the closing would go smoothly.

Wondering if she'd finished everything was one of Liz's most common thought patterns. Sometimes she sat up straight in bed at night, convinced she'd forgotten to attend all the classes she needed to attend in college, even though she had a diploma. When she got married a dozen years ago, she was still thinking of items to cross off her "to do" list when she was on her honeymoon. Having two kids and a husband who primarily worked overseas had added to the anxiety level, as did her job. Working around other people's schedules for showings, answering hundreds of questions, and dealing with all the details of her position kept her in a constant state of motion when she was at work. The stress level didn't diminish at home.

When they arrived at the retirement home, Liz was glad the other three little girls were enthusiastic about their mission. She would have had to coax Jessica out of the car otherwise, but Jess was going along with the program to fit in.

There were 16 children in all, and the performance went well. About 40 residents assembled in the center's large living room to hear the kids sing. The room was decorated tastefully in rich burgundy, cream, gold, and sage green. Two large brass candelabra lighting fixtures hung from the ceiling. Several sofas, armchairs, and end tables defined specific seating areas. Some of the residents sat on brown metal folding chairs the staff had brought in to supplement the seating, while several residents were in wheelchairs.

A black grand piano stood in one corner of the room. A large vase filled with spring flowers was on top of it. The arrangement included waxy white, pink and purple hyacinths that perfumed the whole room.

Mrs. Miller, the choir director, played the piano most often during the performance, but Jessica and one other girl accompanied the group on two songs. "Jesus Loves Me" was recognizable, so Liz, Jessica, and Mrs. Miller were pleased.

Afterwards, the kids shyly served the Girl Scout cookies to the residents, as well as punch in blue, disposable plastic cups. Some of the residents were pleased to accept the refreshments, while others didn't take anything, or just stared blankly at the kids.

Liz was within earshot when Jessica approached one lady in a wheelchair. The woman had snow-white hair that was styled nicely. She wore a white blouse, a navy blue skirt, and black, orthopedic shoes over pantyhose. A pearl necklace and pearl clip earrings complimented her ensemble. She had a hump in her back from osteoporosis and she wore a hearing aid, but her eyes were bright and she was smiling.

"Would you like a cupcake and punch?" Jessica asked, moving her blond bangs out of her eyes with a swipe of her tiny hand.

"Just the drink, please," the woman responded, taking the cup from her. "You're one of the little girls who played the piano, right?"

"Uh-huh," Jessica admitted. "I'm Jessica. My mom makes me take piano lessons."

"That's wonderful!" the lady said. "My name is Mrs. Weber. Learning to play music is something you will enjoy your entire life. I learned to play the piano when I was about your age too."

"You did?" Jessica said. "Can you still play? I thought old folks just sat around all day."

"Yes, I still play," Mrs. Weber said. "Let me put this drink down, and I'll show you."

She put her cup on an end table and maneuvered her wheelchair over to the piano. Jessica pushed the piano bench to the side so the wheelchair would fit, and sat on it.

Mrs. Weber played a few bars of "Chopsticks" as a tease, and then filled the room with a classical composition complete with many difficult passages.

The other residents knew what to expect, but Jessica, Liz, and the rest of the choir were in awe.

"That's a little Beethoven," Mrs. Weber said when she finished. "Now I'll give you a little Mozart."

Once again, she performed the difficult music from memory.

"You're good," Jessica told her when she finished.

"You can be good too; you just have to practice," Mrs. Weber told her. "I still practice, almost every day."

"You do?" Jessica said. "I hate to practice."

"It gets more fun as you go along," Mrs. Weber assured her.

"What else do you do for fun?" Jess wanted to know.

"Oh, I play cards and board games, and I knit and read a lot," Mrs. Weber said. "Sometimes I play the piano and read to the other residents here. I keep busy."

"Wow," Jessica said. "I thought people in old folks' homes just sat around and waited to die."

Liz, who had been eavesdropping, was mortified, but Mrs. Weber took it in stride.

"I'm not waiting to die," she said. "Everyone will die someday, but we should live life to the fullest each day we can. We all have gifts we should share, too."

"I don't want to die. I don't want you to die, either," Jessica said solemnly.

"Thank you, child, but it's in God's hands," Mrs. Weber responded. "I don't even think about it much, because I'm too busy."

"Do you have any children?" Jessica wanted to know. "I guess they'd be grown-ups now though."

"No, I never had any children, and my husband, Donald, passed away 15 years ago," Mrs. Weber said. "I was very sad, and I could have given up, but instead I found new things to do. I am always learning something. I'd like to take a dance class, but I can't because of the wheelchair. However, I do chair yoga, and in two weeks I'm starting a watercolor painting class."

"Wow!" Jessica said, impressed. "I like to finger paint," she noted. "But you don't have any family to visit you?" she pressed.

"No," Mrs. Weber admitted.

Liz couldn't believe the next exchange.

"I want you to keep my reindeer, Ginger," Jessica said. "I love him, but I want him to stay with you."

She went to her backpack and pulled out her favorite stuffed animal, which had been her constant companion since she first laid eyes on him. She had immediately named him Ginger, although she also always referred to the toy as a "him" despite his feminine name. She pressed Ginger into Mrs. Weber's lap, and gave him one last pat.

"Oh, Honey, no!" Mrs. Weber said, surprised with the gift. "You need to keep Ginger."

"No, I want him to keep you company," Jessica said firmly. "I don't want you to be alone. I'll ask my mom if we can come back and visit you both."

Later, when Liz was driving the three neighbor girls and Jessica home, Liz thought about the afternoon. The whole experience had touched her.

Our culture is fascinated with youth, but our senior citizens can teach us all so much she thought. *Why isn't my Facebook timeline filled with pictures of amazing senior citizens as much as it is with kids and pets? We shouldn't throw these people away; they have so much to give if we would all slow down and enjoy them.*

And slowing down is something I need to do more of too, she added to herself.

13

Bobby Gaines' Excellent Restart

Bobby Gaines went down a few steps and into the pit area at Williams Grove Speedway, being careful not to fall. The left heel of his new work boots was higher than the right one to compensate for his now-permanent limp, and he wasn't used to them yet. He didn't want anyone to know he usually used a cane for support, so he'd left it in his pickup.

Bobby knew attending his first race after the accident that had changed his life would be difficult, but the flood of emotions he was dealing with made him want to return to the parking lot and drive away, never to return. He had almost died in a sprint car accident here a couple of years ago when he flipped out of the ballpark between Turns 1 and 2. Miraculously he'd lived, but beating his addiction to his pain medication had been as challenging as healing from his physical injuries. Both had changed his life forever.

Now, instead of getting ready for warm-ups as he'd done here so many Friday nights in the past, Bobby was just one of many people who strolled the pits before the races, visiting with old friends and nodding to acquaintances. Considering his former position as one of the most promising young drivers in the country, it felt wrong not to be getting ready to go onto the track.

It was nice to be remembered, though, and nearly everyone in the pits remembered Bobby Gaines. He shook so many hands and got so many claps on the back of his red-and-black racing jacket, he felt like a politician at a convention. He had put on a little weight, and his blue eyes were always tired now since he could never get comfortable enough to sleep for long. He wore his blond hair in the same style, though, and his smile was still bright.

The following day was St. Patrick's Day, and there was a definite party atmosphere in the infield. Bobby knew the guys on Beer Hill would be enjoying their beer, even if there was a chill in the evening air of Central Pennsylvania in the early spring. Some fans wore green, a color Bobby was far too superstitious to wear to an oval-track race.

"Hey there, Druggy," said a familiar voice behind him. He would have taken exception to the nickname referring to his excessive popping of pills if it hadn't come from Trevor Anthony, one of the few drivers who had visited him in the hospital. Most drivers didn't mind visiting sick kids in the hospital, but it was harder to visit one of their own who was doing sheet time. It was too much of a reminder they could be in the same position at any time.

But Trevor had come to the hospital twice. The first time Bobby was still unconscious, but the second time he'd relished the visit from his friend, who brought gifts of the latest copy of "Speed Sport Magazine," a paddle ball toy, and two cans of Silly String they had used on each other before Trevor left.

"Trevor," Bobby responded. "Have you picked your gears yet, or are you as clueless as usual?"

"Now you know they never let me do that," Trevor said, smiling. "I'm just supposed to get in, shut up, and drive. But it's great to see you!" he added earnestly.

"It's great to be seen, I think," Bobby replied.

Attending this race hadn't been high on his list, but Emily, one of the girls who worked in timing and scoring, had talked him into it. He moved on down the line of sprint cars, stopping to speak to various people around each car. He loved the smell of clay mixed with tire rubber and methanol, the loud thunder of the engines, and the colorful colors of the cars, especially at night as they shimmered when they passed the large lights illuminating the track. In one way it was medicine for his soul, but it was accompanied by a feeling of deep loss. Bobby had worked hard to make a name for himself as a sprint car driver, but his career had been over in less than a minute, and he had paid a high price for his involvement in the sport.

When he reached Turn 4, Bobby turned and retraced his path back to Trevor's car. The sunset was spectacular, as pink and orange streaks highlighted where the cornfields met the sky. The infield sported uneven clumps of tender green grass that had not yet undergone their first mowing of the year.

"You can watch from the top of the transporter if you want," Trevor said right before he climbed into the cockpit of his car. "Make yourself at home."

Bobby nodded, and looked at the narrow metal ladder attached to the side of the big white transporter. Before the accident, he would have scaled it in a few quick movements, holding on with just one hand and carrying a couple of collapsible lawn chairs in the other. He didn't want to admit it to Trevor, but he knew he couldn't climb it anymore, especially not in these boots.

He helped push Trevor's car back out of its space in the pits so it could get lined up for a push truck. Right before Trevor went out for warm-ups, Bobby leaned into the cockpit to speak to his friend.

"I'm going to watch from the stands," he said. "Good luck!"

Trevor nodded through his visor and tear-offs, and less than a minute later he was on the half-mile oval.

Bobby turned and went out of the pits. Before heading for the tunnel under Turn 1, he stopped at the ambulance parked in the infield to thank the emergency workers for their help after his crash.

They recognized him immediately.

"We were just doing our job," one said, "but thanks for stopping by. It means a lot. We took one look at you that night and we knew our main job was to try to get you stable and ready for the helicopter. That was one nasty crash. It's great to see you back at the races!"

Bobby thanked them again, and walked toward the tunnel under the track. The ground was a little wet at both ends of it, and he was careful not to slip.

Once on the other side, he paused a minute, divided. Most of him wanted to proceed to the parking lot and head home. It was too hard to watch other people do what he should be doing but no longer could. But he'd come this far, it was a nice night for the middle of March, and he didn't want to have to admit to Emily he had left early, so he proceeded past the office to the frontstretch grandstands and found a seat.

Trevor was already back in the pits before Bobby was settled. The heats went off with only two cautions, and Bobby was pleased when a family a few rows above him recognized him and sent their little boy down for his autograph.

His back hurt from the hardness of his seat, and all his muscles were stiff. He took a restroom break during intermission, and when he headed back to where he had been sitting, he heard his name called out. It was Old Man Saunders, a local sprint car owner who had offered him a ride in his World of Outlaws sprint car right before the accident. When Bobby was hurt, he'd abandoned his plans for going out on the road. As far as Bobby knew, his equipment was still sitting in a garage someplace, unused. He knew many drivers would have been after the ride, but Old Man Saunders was famous for only doing things if and when he wanted to.

Al Saunders motioned for Bobby to sit with him.

He didn't have to ask twice.

"How are you doing, Bobby?" said Al, pointing towards a spot beside him to his left on a long, red-plaid blanket he had stretched over the bleacher seats. "Have a seat."

"Better, thank you," Bobby said, shaking Al's hand. "It's been a long time. This is my first race since the accident."

"Bobby, this is my friend, Gary Griffith," Al said, motioning to a man on his right. Bobby recognized him as the owner of a large trucking company who sponsored some races.

"Pleased to meet you," Bobby said, shaking Gary's hand too.

"It's good to see you," Al said earnestly. He wore a thick black jacket embroidered with the name of one of his car dealerships on the back. He was wearing a cap advertising another one of them, and he had a black scarf and soft, black leather gloves to ward against the cold. He had gray hair, but he was so fit he looked younger than his actual age of 70.

The pair shared more small talk but had to stop due to the noise of the cars in the consy.

They picked up again between the consy and the feature.

Linda Mansfield

"Are you working?" Al wanted to know.

"Not yet," Bobby admitted. "I need a job, but I haven't had time to look for one. I went through a pretty extensive rehab program, and I'm still in a pain-management program. I'm getting a handle on it, but there are days where the pain is so bad I can't even get out of bed. But I finally found a good pain-management clinic. They don't have to be certified, so there's a big difference in what's available out there. This one offers lots of different options."

"I see," Al said. "I'm sure it's a process."

"Yeah; I got addicted to my pain meds, and getting that regulated took a 12-step program. But I'm doing much better now."

"I heard the gossip," Al said. "It's great to see you out at the races again though."

"Thanks," Bobby said. "It's hard to be here without driving, but I have to accept that racing is in my past."

Al didn't say anything, and soon they couldn't talk anyway due to the blare of the announcer over the loudspeakers and the cars warming up for the feature.

"Who do you think will win?" Al asked him when there was a moment quiet enough to talk.

"Justin and Lucas are always good here, and Trevor ran well in his heat," Bobby said. "Nelson is on the pole, but he gets too excited when he has a good starting spot. He'll be no better than fourth by lap two."

He was right. Nelson went backwards, Justin won, Lucas was second, and Trevor finished third.

Most of the crowd left immediately after the sprint car feature because by that time it was cold. Gary told Al and Bobby goodbye and headed for an exit. Al tarried a bit, and Bobby followed his lead.

"Right before your accident, I asked you to come see me so we

110

could go Outlaw racing," Al said. "I know you couldn't keep that appointment, but I'm going to suggest you think about coming to see me next week," he said. "I'd still like to go Outlaw racing."

Then he posed an interesting question.

"I know you're not up to driving, but what about being my team manager?" Al suggested.

Bobby looked at him, dumbfounded. He'd been concentrating on everything he'd lost and the disappointment of not driving anymore, and hadn't imagined a different role in the sport he loved.

"To start with, you'll have to try to come up with some sponsorship money, because I'd rather not foot the whole bill myself," Al continued. "I don't want to pay you for the days you can't get out of bed either, so you'll have to punch a time clock like one of my mechanics," he added with a twinkle in his eye. "But you'd be back in racing full-time."

Suddenly, Bobby wasn't feeling sorry for himself.

"That's an awesome opportunity, Mr. Saunders," he said. "Thank you! I know I'd like to try."

"Be at my office at 9 a.m. Monday morning, and we'll get started," Al said, pleased. "There's a lot of work to do. I have some ideas, and I'm sure you will too."

"Yes! Thank you very, very much!" Bobby said. "I won't let you down!"

Al smiled, shook Bobby's hand, stood, and folded his blanket.

"Now are you glad you came?" he said.

"Yes, sir!" Bobby said, happier than he'd been in ages. It might not be the leprechaun's proverbial pot of gold at the end of the rainbow, but it was a chance for a new beginning he wasn't going to waste.

About the Author

Linda Mansfield is an award-winning reporter, editor, author, and public relations representative. She is a former editor at a Manhattan publishing house. She was the first female editorial staff member of "National Speed Sport News," and her work appears regularly in its successor, "Speed Sport Magazine." She owns Restart Communications, a public relations agency based in Indianapolis.

Her first collection of fictional short stories, "Stories for the 12 Days of Christmas," debuted in 2015. In 2017 she is releasing three sequels: "Twelve Stories for Spring," "Twelve Stories for Summer," and "Twelve Stories for Fall." All four books stand alone; there are no cliffhangers or "to be continued" lines.

Mansfield's family has grown since her last book and now includes one horse, one dog, and four cats. She doesn't currently have any fish, although she used to have a small aquarium and she has enjoyed fishing in the past, as shown in the accompanying photo taken during a long-ago spring. She has several things in common with the character Lucy who you met in the eighth story in this book, "Soul Food."

To learn of Mansfield's upcoming releases by e-mail, readers are encouraged to subscribe to her e-mail list through her Web site at

LindaMansfieldBooks.com, and receive a free short story as her thank you.

Readers may also reach her on Facebook at "Linda Mansfield — Author," and at Twitter at @RestartLMAuthor. She has a YouTube channel and a blog too.

Reviews are very important to authors. If you liked "Twelve Stories for Spring," Mansfield would be grateful if you'd leave a positive review on the Web site of the outlet where you purchased it.

Linda Mansfield, not quite 5 years old, and her big catch.

Don't miss the other books
in the "Two Good Feet" series!

1
Available now!

2
Available now!

3
Summer of '17

4
Fall of '17

www.ingramcontent.com/pod-product-compliance
Lightning Source LLC
Chambersburg PA
CBHW031839170626
46807CB00004B/1526